# DARK WATER PIRATES

*Story Keeping Series, Book 4*

## A R MARSHALL

D1409114

*For Oliver*
*Your adventurous spirit inspired this tale,*
*& you steadfast courage finished it.*


*For Claire*
*You are ever brave, strong, & confident.*


*For Sam & Maria*
*May your training as Story Keepers continue.*
*Riles, Sissie, & Finn will need your help!*

# FREE AUDIO BOOK

Thanks for checking out the Story Keeping Series. You're going to love it. As a token of thanks, download a free copy of the audiobook for the first in this series - The Night I Became A Hero.

Click on the image or URL below for access:
https://storykeeping.carrd.co

## PRAISE FOR A. R. MARSHALL'S STORY KEEPING SERIES

My 11y son has been plowing through this set and is asking for more. This set of books has made him want to read and not play video games all day.

— RHONDA

My son, age 10, loves the story line! Perfect for the reluctant reader that hasn't found their "love" for reading yet. After reading book one, he has been reading and reading!!

— KATHRENE

My son is in love, so happy to find a quality adventure book that keeps him reading.

— MELINDA

# CONTENTS

PROLOGUE

**H**i. My name is Riles.

Just in case you missed my first three stories - or maybe you read them a long time ago - here's a little bit about me so you feel caught up.

I am a hero. So are my sister and brother.

We can't fly. We don't have super speed, x-ray vision, plastic arms, or super strength. In fact, we're pretty normal in every way except one – we are *Story Keepers*.

Have you ever heard of a *Story Keeping*? That's okay, neither had we - until that first summer at grandpa's house.

Ever since I can remember, Sissie, Finn and I get to spend a week each summer at grandpa's house.

Mom and dad drop us off at the beginning of the week and pick us up seven days later. Over the years, we've had amazing adventures with grandpa – treasure hunts, night hikes, star-gazing, and s'mores around the back-yard fire pit.

This summer grandpa took the adventures to a whole new level.

He introduced us to story keeping. You know how most stories have happy endings? I love rooting for happy endings.

Well, happy endings need help? Happy endings aren't guaranteed.

There are people out there, right now, trying to ruin stories by taking away the happy ending. Crazy, right?

Grandpa says people have been saving stories for centuries. His mom trained him to be a *Story Keeper*, and she learned *Story Keeping* from her great uncles.

When stories need saving, *Story Keepers* take action. I know, it sounds kind of silly, but it's true. We protect stories and save happy endings.

A few days ago we had our first adventure, saving Drift Elwick from a mess of trouble on a spaceship parked between Earth and Mars. Then, I almost got stuck in the middle ages with a nasty magician and a whiny prince, but Sissie found a way to help me home.

Today, we helped Charlotte discover treasure along the Nile and protect an ancient secret. We also found out - spoiler alert - our parents are story keepers too!

It would probably help if I reminded you where our last story ended. Sissie had just returned from Charlotte's book when we heard a loud "thud" in the basement.

It shook the house.

We froze. Grandpa listened.

We thought it might be father. He had helped Sissie in Charlotte's book. Maybe he had returned? Somehow?

Grandpa had a curious look on his face – serious and maybe a bit concerned.

He stood up from the table and grabbed a frying pan in the kitchen. Holding it like a sword, he headed down the hall, toward the basement. We followed close behind.

Sissie grabbed my arm and squeezed it tight. Little Finn tucked in behind grandpa's leg.

He always locked the basement door.

Grandpa dug a bulky keychain out of his pocket, slide the keys between his fingers, and selected one. He fit the key into the lock and turned it.

None of us had ever been down there before. I could hear my own heart pounding faster than normal.

The door stuck a bit and then creaked open.

Cold air snuck up the staircase, raising goose-bumps up and down my arms. It smelled musty like old books and camping gear. We heard quiet whispering in the room below.

Tiptoeing, we following grandpa one step at a time - through the doorway and down the steep wooden steps. At every creak, grandpa paused to listen before continuing.

Then, the whispers stopped.

We froze.

Suddenly, a bright white flash filled the stairwell.

Grandpa hustled down the last few steps and turned into the basement. We followed closely, not wanting to be left behind.

Grandpa moved quickly toward a square, wooden table in the center of the room. Two open books glowed on the table top, and two mugs rested to the side, still steaming. Two chairs had been pushed back from the table.

Standing over the table, grandpa chuckled softly and let out a sigh.

"What in the world do they think they're doing?" he whispered, loud enough for us to hear.

"They?" I whispered back.

"Your parents."

Grandpa flipped the first book closed. We recognized the sandy brown binding and thick border of hieroglyphs at once.

They had been reading Charlotte's story.

What will the rest of the week hold? Well, keep reading - you'll see. These adventures get crazier with every passing hour. That's why storytime is still my favorite part of the day.

## FINN'S FOLLY

A fternoon light filtered into the basement. Grandpa sat in one of the open chairs at the square table. He slowly stroked his chin, thinking, while steam rose from two mugs on the table - our parent's mugs.

Two books also sat on the table. Charlotte's book, rested closed in front of grandpa. On the other side of the table, bubbling bright light rose from a second, open book.

The basement looked a bit like a 1940's military bunker. Giant, old rugs covered most of the cement floor. Shelves stuffed with books lined two of the walls – their bindings represented all kinds of shapes, sizes, and colors.

Sissie, Finn, and I watched grandpa for a few

moments. Now that we felt safe again - knowing our parents made the terrifying "thud," we started exploring the room.

Finn ran straight to the bookcases – hoping to find more glowing books.

Sissie drifted behind grandpa, toward a rolling chalkboard covered edge to edge in unfamiliar mathematical equations and strange symbols.

My eyes traveled to another wall. It was covered in photos, maps, and newspaper clippings. Below the collage, was a desk covered in disorganized paper piles mixed with old books.

I headed that direction to explore.

Lots of the paper had handwritten notes on it. I recognized grandpa's writing on some of the papers. Others looked like mom and dad's writing. Still others looked like pages torn from old books, or written on a typewriter.

Highlights, pen marks, and underlines filled the different pages spread out across the desk. Sometimes notes filled the margins.

You could hardly see the desk beneath the loose papers and books.

The books looked special – and really old. None of them seemed to glow, but I didn't want to touch them just in case.

What did it all mean? My mind raised with excitement and curiosity.

Grandpa remained in his chair at the table, still thinking and watching as we explored.

Underneath the desk I found several cardboard boxes stuffed with electronics – circuits and fuses wired this way and that, radios and phones pieced apart and strung back together with loose wiring.

My imagination bubbled. Was grandpa building something? Was father or mother?

I looked over at grandpa. He looked up from his thinking and winked at me. *He's letting us explore*, I thought. *What does he want us to find? Another adventure?*

Sissie stepped back from the chalkboard and joined me by the desk. She scanned the wall - a messy collection of maps, photos, and news clips. They hung like flies in a spider web, held up with pins and connected by bits of string hung between the them.

We felt a bit like Nancy Drew or Sherlock Holmes, review clues for a case.

Something tied all these clues together – somehow this wall told a story.

Sissie and I examined the wall clippings in silence. After a few moments, grandpa joined us, standing quietly behind us. Little Finn still seemed content to climb the bookcases.

"Look," I whispered under my breath, raising my hand toward a photo near the top left of the wall.

It looked like a photo of an old book store. I spotted Drift's book, on the shelf in the picture. A leather book propped up, revealing planets on its cover.

I smiled. That book represented our first story keeping adventure. Was it really just a few days ago that I met Drift? Incredible. In less than a week, my hold world had spun upside down.

My finger followed the red piece of string as it stretched from that photo to a newspaper clipping – some kind of advertisement:

"Seekers and Keepers another calling is found. Leather bound, $500."

"Five-hundred dollars?" Sissie whispered. "That's an expensive book."

"It's a special one, as you know," grandpa whispered from behind us.

My finger traced another string – one connecting the advertisement to a city map. The map showed a city full of winding roads and large parks. Lots of strings stretched like sun rays from that city map.

"That must be an important city," I whispered.

"Uh-huh," She whispered back.

Grandpa sighed, lost in memories of his own.

"Is that mom and dad?" Sissie asked, pointing toward the middle of the wall.

"I think so, but that must have been taken a long time ago," I whispered back.

"Yes," grandpa said quietly, "just after your parents met, at university."

I wondered, *Did mom and dad know about story keeping way back then?*

My eyes drifted from that picture to so many others – strings linking people and articles, books, and maps.

One, a picture of a girl and an older man walking in a park, caught my attention. It was faded and a bit blurry. The man wore a long dark coat and a hat that shadowed his face. The girl looked familiar. Could it be?

"Lark?" The name slipped out under my breath. Only Sissie heard it.

She looked at me and then scanned the wall.

"You're right, it is her," she whispered back.

I nodded, my eyes still holding on to the photo.

"Grandpa, who are these people? What is all this?" the words snuck out of my throat in another whisper.

He looked toward the picture of the man and the girl.

"Do you recognize them?" he replied quietly.

"Yes, well, some of them."

I did. I just couldn't believe it.

What was a picture of Lark doing in my grandpa's basement? And, who was the man walking with her in the park?

"The girl looks like Lark," Sissie whispered.

Grandpa nodded, "That's correct."

"Did you take that photo?" I asked.

"No."

"Did you put all this stuff on the wall?" I asked.

"Some of it," grandpa replied cautiously.

As we whispered, little Finn joined us.

"What is all this?" he asked in his best attempt at a whisper.

"Children," grandpa started in, "you are only just starting to learn about story keeping. I'm sure you have lots of questions. It will take time for you to find all your answers.

"But you've been teaching us all week?" Sissie interrupted.

"Elizabeth, my dear" grandpa answered gently, "It's only been a few days since our first story. You're only beginning to understand - only beginning to meet our friends, and foes."

"I haven't met anyone," Finn blurted out, "because you won't let me in any stories."

Grandpa placed his hand on Finn's shoulder, "Dear little Finn, you are still young. Don't be in such a hurry to grow up."

Finn huffed, "I just want to go on an adventure like everyone else."

Pouting, he folded his arms and headed back to the bookcase. Grandpa sighed, as Finn stomped off.

"It looks like your father and mother have moved into another story."

Sissie and I exchanged glances as we listened.

"I didn't expect them to visit Charlotte's story," he went on, "but I'm sure they have their reasons."

"You think they jumped into the other book?" I asked.

"I believe so."

Though we didn't know it at the time, little Finn heard grandpa.

"Can we read it?" Sissie asked.

Though we didn't see it at the time, curiosity drove little Finn toward the square table - toward the open, glowing book.

"I'm not sure that's a good idea," grandpa said, lowering his voice. "It's not a very safe book."

"Did you say father and mother jumped into this book?" Finn called at us from the center of the room.

Grandpa, Sissie and I spun around to see Little

Finn standing on a chair, leaning on the table, hovering over the open book.

"Finn, wait, what are you doing?" I called.

"I'm tired of not having my own adventure," Finn whined. "I going after mom and dad."

"Finn don't!" grandpa shouted, lunging for the table, but it was too late. In a flash of white, little Finn was gone.

## 2

## INTO DARK WATER

**G**randpa rushed across the room.

Frozen, Sissie and I looked at each other with wild eyes.

*Did that really just happen?*

Grandpa leaned over the glowing book ‑ his eyes scanning the pages, his voice silent.

"Grandpa, what's happening!" Sissie blurted.

Grandpa's brow furrowed as he studied the open pages.

We rushed beside him.

"Grandpa, what's going on?" Sissie whispered.

He kept reading to himself.

"Out loud, please!" I urged.

Grandpa ignored us.

Then, leaning back from the book he nodded to himself and mumbled, "Hmm."

Sissie and I waited for more.

"I suppose it could be worse," grandpa continued, more to himself than us.

"Please, grandpa?" Sissie said again, tugging at his arm.

"Yes, yes of course," grandpa said, looking up. "Sorry children. It's just that this book can be, well, a bit tricky."

"Tricky?" I asked, still nervous and confused.

"Yes, tricky," Grandpa repeated. "But Finn's okay, for the time being, I'm quite sure of that."

My shoulders rolled back. Sissie tried to relax - letting go of grandpa's arm. "Okay" was good news, even if it was temporary.

"Shall we settle in down here," grandpa continued, "and start reading?"

Sissie and I both nodded. We pulled several chairs across the basement so we could sit on either side of grandpa at the square table.

"Ready?" he asked, with a slight shake in his voice.

Okay or not, grandpa still seemed nervous. We just wanted Finn home and safe.

"I'll back up a bit so you can hear the part I've already read."

We nodded.

The glowing pages fluttered as grandpa began.

DARK SKY MET DARK WATER. Between the sound of creaking wood and crashing waves, hollow shouts interrupted the darkness.

"Pull the sails. Settled the lines!" a voice called from the helm.

"Ay, captain!" a team of voices echoed above shifting winds.

As the Starling tossed about in massive waves, her mast leaned to and fro. Her crew raced like rats across her dark deck, lit only occasionally by flashes of lightening. The sailors scurried, securing her lines and pulling in her sails. High winds tossed angry waves at the tall ship. Sideways rain pelted the crew. The unexpected storm was upon them.

"Quick ye scabbards, hold the lines, secure the cargo!" the Captain's voice pierced through the darkness.

Ay, captain!" the crew called again.

Then, a voice called down from the crow's nest, "Captain quick!"

"Ay?"

"Somethin' strange and small be tossin' in the starboard waves."

The captain moved quickly, from helm to bow. He was tall and sturdy, walking steadily despite the shifting deck. He carried a lantern glowing gold, the only light across the wide horizon. As he moved, the sway of light exposed his drenched frame, strong beard of red, and bright blue eyes. His broad hat sagged under the weight of rainwater as he leaned over the Starling's rail.

Holding the lantern high in his outstretched arm, he scanned the angry sea.

Shafts of light reached beyond the deck, casting shadows into the shifting waves and driving rain.

Nothing.

"There captain, toward the fourth star," the voice from the nest.

Captain Red Beard moved ten steps to the bow and raised the lantern to his right. Then, between waves and rain, he saw what the watchman had called out - a small something. Was it a body?

"Ay, there it is," he cried out.

The ship creaked, tossed forward by the taunting storm. Several of the crew fell flat on the deck, surprised and caught off balance. But not the captain.

Red Beard stood firm, gripping a line, and holding the lantern high.

"Looks to be a lifeless life, boys," his commanding voice rose above the sounds of the storm. "Fish it out and quick. Never know what we might be findin'. Strange things happen in these seas boys, strange things."

Before he had finished speaking, two of the crew leapt into the water holding lines. Two others tied down the other end of each line, ready to retrieve their shipmates. In moments, they had the body on deck.

"He looks to be breathin'," Captain Red Beard chuckled dismissively. "Perhaps the prince has smiled on this one - lost in the dark water.

"Ay, to Bright Water," the crew cheered as they raised their swords in salute, "to the Prince."

The captain's eyes glowed, "Toss him in the brig'. When the storm passes, we'll be havin' some words with this lit'le one."

Two mates sheathed their swords, lifted the unconscious body from the deck, and dragged him below.

There was little time to rest. The storm raged on. The hull of the ship tossed up again, creaking as thrashing waves squeezed her wooden rails from either side. Steady as ever, Captain Red Beard made his way back to the helm. Slashing rain continued pelting his sturdy frame. Yet, he stood strong behind the wheel, still holding the lantern high.

"Tie down the lines boys!" he shouted. "She's holdin' well, and this storm 'ill be by us in no time."

"Ay Captain!" they hollered back from all corners of the deck.

"Is that body Finn?" I interrupted, stunned.

"Not sure yet," grandpa paused, "but I think so."

*You think so?* I thought. *How is this okay?*

"How could it possibly be worse?" Sissie looked up from the table with deep concern.

"Well, he's alive, and he's below deck," grandpa spoke carefully, in a soft tone.

After an awkward pause, I spoke up: "Grandpa, keep reading. I think Finn's going to need our help."

Grandpa nodded, and continued to read.

Below deck, several hanging lanterns glowed dim, casting shadows about, mirroring the violent sway of the sea.

Eventually, the storm passed, just as the Captain predicted. The once empty brig' now held its first prisoner since the early days. Two shipmates held watch, seated on wooden stools in a small hallway between iron gated cells.

Behind one set of bars, the lifeless life lay still.

## 3

# LUCKY TO LIVE

The boat settled into its usual rock as the sea calmed. Still, the two shipmates watched the cell.

"Lucky bloke," one mate said to the other.

"Ya think so, Lucky?" said the other.

"Ay, I do," Lucky replied.

"Supposin' I thought he warn't so lucky, Lucky. Supposin' I dis'greed wi'ch ya. Ya t'ink ya could explain to me why ya be callin' it lucky to be found nearly drowned in the middle of the dark sea, in the middle of a dark storm? Seems everyt'ing but lucky to me."

Lucky chuckled. "Listen, he be lucky 'cause he be breathin' – he be livin' when he should'a'bin dyin'. An' anyone 'ould be happier livin' than dyin', right?"

"Ay, I suppose ya be right," Freckles sighed. "But livin' on dis boat ain't no easy livin'."

Lucky rubbed his furry blonde chin and looked down at his wooden leg. Just the sight of it made him smile. He started tapping it against the floorboards, setting a pace.

"Now what are ya doin'?" Freckles complained.

Lucky winked at Freckles and started slapped a rhythm on his knee.

"Don't ya start wit' that singin' again!"

Lucky winked again and began humming a song from the old days.

Freckles shook his head, and shoved Lucky off his stool.

Lucky laughed as he fell, "Ay, music always makes ya smile, even when ya don't think you want to be smilin'."

"Wait, so those two guys are waiting for Finn to wake up?" Sissie interrupted, "And he's in jail on their ship?"

"Looks that way," grandpa replied.

"We need to get in there!" Sissie urged, "We need to help him."

"I don't know," I smiled, "they don't sound so bad.

Do we need to be worried? I mean, Finn really wanted to get in a story, right?"

Sissie shot me a look, "They threw him in jail, Riles!"

"Easy you two," grandpa jumped in, "let's get back to the story so we can help Finn."

We both nodded, and grandpa continued to read.

FROM THE GROUND, Lucky kept tapping his peg against the floorboards and started to hum a jig.

Inside the iron cell, the lifeless life coughed. Lucky kept humming.

"Knock off that ridiculous racket," Freckles hollered at Lucky.

Lucky pulled himself up, still humming, and started to dance - tapping his peg against the floor to keep the beat.

The boy inside the cell coughed again, but neither sailor noticed.

Lucky continued to hum and dance.

Freckles jumped up too, and lunged at Lucky to tackle him. As he leapt, the ship tossed left in a wave. Lucky swung left, holding iron bars for balance.

Freckles landed hard on the stiff floorboards with a groan.

"GRANDPA, NOW'S OUR CHANCE," Sissie interrupted.

"For what?" I asked.

"To send Finn a message," Sissie snapped back.

Grandpa frowned at Sissie's tone, but the book glowed bright at her suggestion.

"What are you going to tell him?" I asked. "He's gonna wake up in jail and we don't actually know what's going on!"

Sissie shot me a sassy, sideways glance.

Looking at the book, she blurted: "We've got your back Little Finn!"

The book glowed bright. The message was sent.

I rolled my eyes and turned back to grandpa, "Can we get back to the story?"

"Both of you need to settle down a bit," grandpa sighed. "We aren't going to get through this story without some teamwork."

Sissie and I glared at each other, still upset. Getting along would take more time.

We stubbornly nodded "okay" to grandpa and he continued reading.

※

LUCKY CHUCKLED at Freckles crumpled on the floor.

"Not yer day again, ay Freckles?" he said through the laughter, still tapping his peg leg to the beat in his head.

"If ya so much as hum another bar o' that tune," Freckles steamed from the ground, "so help me, I'll rip yer lips right off ya face!"

"Ya seem extra rotten grumpy today, Freckles," Lucky smile, poking at Freckles with his peg.

As the two sailors bickered, a small piece of torn white paper appeared at the ceiling and drifted to the floor, resting beside the lifeless life in the cell.

The boy coughed again.

This time Lucky heard it, spinning around to face the cell. Freckles, who rarely missed opportunities like this, spun to his knees and tackled Lucky. The two wrestled for a few moments, shouting bits and pieces at one another.

Through it all Lucky continued to laugh, driving Freckles mad.

As they tussled, the boy woke. After a few more coughs, he rolled to his knees and rubbed his eyes. When he saw the wrestling sailors, he slid backward into the shadows.

"Get yer han's off me you sticky pile of salty seaweed!" Freckles hollered, swinging wildly at Lucky.

Lucky, who somehow had the upper hand, continued to laugh as he pinned Freckles against the floor. The laughter made Freckles more and more angry, and the screaming continued.

Just before Lucky started humming again, a stampede of footsteps raced down the stairs.

"What in blazes are ye two knuckle-headed sea urchins doing!"

Freckles and Lucky froze, looking over their shoulders to see a fierce Captain Red Beard standing firm in the narrow hallway. The boy watched from the shadows.

"Right, sorry Captain," Lucky muttered. "This one's in another one of his moods."

"He won't stop wit' his ridiculous hummin'," Freckles whined.

"Stop it, both of you, you slimy sea cucumbers!" the Captain hollered. "Have you even bin watchin' da lifeless life I sent ya do'n here to watch?"

"Ay, Captain," Freckles answered, "He's still sleeping right," but as he pointed, he realized the body was gone.

Lucky started to laugh, but a quick glance from the Captain silenced him.

Red Beard shook his head at Freckles, and turned to the cell. Grabbing onto the iron bars and leaning in, the Captain's clear blue eyes caught the stare of a shivering boy hiding in the shadows.

"So, sailor," Red Beard whispered, "What brings ye to the depths of the dark waters?"

## 4

### LOOKIN' FOR ADVENTURE

Little Finn kept his eyes locked with the Captain's. He had already scanned the room - seen the scene. He had noticed the note on the floor between his toes and the iron gate. A note from home, he hoped.

The Captain's questions hung in the air as the ship rocked lightly on calming seas: "What brings ye to the depths of the dark waters?"

"I be lookin' for adventure," Little Finn whispered in his best pirate accent through sopping clothes and cold shivers.

Captain Red Beard smiled. It had been a long time since he'd fished an adventure seeking boy from the cold dark depths.

The Captain turned to Lucky, "Fetch 'im a thick blanket, dry clothes a pair of me smallest boots."

"Ay, Captain," Lucky smiled, throwing a wink at the boy.

Freckles slumped back into his stool with a sour look on his face.

"Ya see, Freckles," Red Beard spoke loud enough for the boy to hear, "the sea be bringin' us hope after all."

"Ay," Freckles sighed, unconvinced. He twirled the tips of a wavy red mustache between his thumb and forefinger.

Lucky returned swiftly, thump-stepping down the stairs with arms full of dry cloth. Shivering, little Finn pulled himself to his feet. He stepped into the gold glow of lightly rocking lanterns, anxious to warm himself.

Lucky slid the heap of cloth through the iron bars and tossed it to the ground. Finn quickly dug in, drying himself and pulling on fresh clothes - a white top, oversized knickers cinched tight with a thick black belt, and a dark blue scarf he used to hold back his wet, moppy hair.

The near fit of each item surprised Finn.

Reaching for the boots, he casually lifted the paper note, slipping it into his pocket. Stepping into the boots Finn felt like the real thing – an honest pirate and a true sailor.

He stepped to the iron gate and again met the Captain's eyes, "Many thanks, Captain."

"It be me pleasure, sailor."

"Now boys," Red Beard said, turning to Lucky and Freckles, "shall we offer our guest a bit 'a hospitality?"

"Ay!" they replied.

"Bring 'im to me quarters," Red Beard said as he turned and headed up the steps.

Freckles stepped forward with a frown, unlocked the gate and tugged at little Finn.

"This way, boy," he muttered.

"Easy mate," Lucky smiled, throwing a wink at Finn, "we best swing 'im by the galley first."

"Ay," Freckles sighed, rolling his eyes.

"WHY HASN'T he read the note yet," Sissie interrupted in her best mom voice.

"Maybe he isn't worried," I replied. "Grandpa, you said this book was dangerous, right?"

"Very."

"So far these guys seem pretty friendly," I went on. "Am I missing something?"

"Always," Sissie snapped.

Grandpa shot a stern look toward both of us and set the book down.

"Listen you two," he said in a calm yet serious voice, "this bickering has got to stop. Your brother is in a story, and he needs you two to support him the same way he supported you. I wouldn't have let him into this story, but he's in it now, so pull it together. Got it?"

"Yes grandpa," we whispered. "Sorry."

"I forgive you both," he smiled. "Now, shall we continue?"

We nodded, and he picked the book back up.

LUCKY AND FRECKLES led Finn up the steps to a middle deck which offered a bit more natural light. Near center ship, they closed in on a tight kitchen.

"Hungry?" Lucky asked.

"Yes, I mean Ay!" Finn replied.

Lucky chuckled, "Good."

Ahead of them, a thick chef muttered behind hot pots and sizzling pans. Behind him, strange roots and salted meat were neatly cut and piled.

Freckles hollered at the chef, "Mutton, what delicacy ya plannin' to tickle our t'roats wit' today?"

"For you Freckles?" Chef bellowed with deep laughter.

"Ay," Freckles grunted back, "an' Lucky and the boy."

Mutton turned toward them for the first time, scanned them up and down with his good eye, and bobbed his head up and down.

"I be boilin' just the t'ing for our shiverin' new mate."

Finn smiled, and stepped forward as Mutton dished up a bowl of slop. The smell flooded Finn with memories as hints of pine, orange, cinnamon, and happiness warmed his nose.

"T'anks Chef," Finn said, still trying on his pirate accent.

"Me pleasure lit'le one, and call me Mutton."

"Ay, Mutton," Finn replied.

"T'anks Mutton," Lucky offered, then looking to Freckles and Finn, "Best be headin' to the Captain's quarters."

"Ay," Freckles sighed, hoping this would finally end his babysitting assignment.

The odd trio left the galley and headed up another set

of stairs near the back half of the ship. This time the stairs led to fresh air, as a cool breeze dried soaked sails. The storm had passed - or paused. The water remained dark and thick clouds hung, filling the sky to the horizon.

Crossing the deck, they headed to a door in the stern: the Captain's quarters. Freckles opened the door, and Finn followed Lucky inside.

Red Beard sat behind a heavy wooden desk full of beautiful and detailed carvings. The Captain didn't seem to notice their arrival. All his attention was focused on a small black book. He seemed to read it carefully, slowly turning from one page to the next.

With a slap on the back from Lucky and a nod from Freckles, the two sailors left Finn alone with the Captain.

Finn's gaze swept across the room, taking it all in. Charts, maps, and trinkets filled the space. Shadows danced in the golden light of dim lanterns.

As Finn took in the room, his hand slipped into his pocket.

*The note*, he thought, as his fingers felt the small scrap of paper.

Eyes on the captain, Finn cautiously unfolded the paper and lifted it out of his pocket.

Without looking up, Red Beard spoke.

## ⚜ 5 ⚜

## CAPTAIN RED BEARD

"**G**o on," Red Beard said, "I be wonderin' what that tiny paper says too."

Little Finn froze.

"Dat tiny paper ya snatched from the cell floor," Red Beard went on, "I be wonderin' what dat tiny paper be sayin'."

Finn shoved the note back in his pocket.

"Go on, read it aloud, boy."

Finn's cheeks turned red. He slowly pulled the note back out and read it softly:

*We've got your back Little Finn.*

"Lit'le Finn?" Red Beard chuckled. "Is that what they call ya?"

"Ay."

Red Beard stood, walked casually around the desk, and sat right on top of it, swinging his big black boots.

"It's a right friendly name, it is," he smiled, "Lit'le Finn."

Finn looked down at his own boots, feeling small. His face felt warm.

"Mutton treat you well?"

"Ay," Finn answered.

"So, Lit'le Finn," Red Beard went on, "It's time ya be sharing' a bit 'a ya'r own story."

He paused, and Finn remained silent.

"Ya know, 'dis arn't da first time a stranger be fallin' into our seas."

Finn looked up slowly, halting as his eyes met the light blues eyes of the captain. Finn saw them sparkle bright.

"Really?" he asked.

"Truly."

Finn took a deep breath and let it out slow. *I'm not alone*, he thought to himself, *I can do this.*

"Captain," Finn said, locking eyes again, "I'm here for adventure, just like I said."

"Ay, I can see that boy," Red Beard smiled. "Ya got a look in yer eyes dat says ya ain't scared 'a nothin'."

Finn cracked a small smile - small but deep. The

captain saw something in Finn that Finn wanted to see in himself.

Suddenly, muffled yelling on deck interrupted the moment.

The door swung open and Lucky leaned in.

"Captain, forgive da interruption."

"Ay."

"Scoop spotted one 'a da govenor's ships off da bow."

"How far?"

"Close," Lucky oozed excitement.

"Sails?"

"Still down from the weather."

"An' he seen da flag?" Red Beard leaned forward, still sitting atop his desk.

"Ay, the black tower."

"An' they ain't seen us?"

"An' she's alone?"

"Ay."

"Make a run an' keep her low. We'll strip her spoils and be off before da sails rise."

"Ay, Captain," Lucky nodded, and shot out of Red Beard's quarters barking orders to the crew.

Red Beard slid forward off the desk and stood facing Finn.

"It's adventure ya be wantin', an' it's adventure ya be gettin'.'"

"Ay, Captain," Finn parroted.

"Ya'll be needin' a sword and a beard."

Finn's face tilted with confusion.

"Ay," Red Beard went on, "ya heard me right. If ya want to be safe, you'll carry a blade. If ya want to join me crew, ya'll need a beard.

"Ay, Captain," Finn barked back.

The longing Finn had felt since they opened the very first story - a longing to participate in something bigger - It was happening. This was his moment, his adventure.

Red Beard moved to a wardrobe tucked behind the quarter's door and began to dig. As he did, they felt the Starling shift direction and catch the wind. Finn swayed a bit and then regained his balance.

The Captain drew out a short blade and sheath.

"Dis blade was me own for a time. Be wise when ye draw her - sometimes she's got a mind of her own."

"Ay," Finn replied, receiving the blade carefully.

Gripping the hilt, Finn swung the sword lightly left and right, feeling the weight and balance of the blade. It felt like part of his hand. An electricity seemed to pulse between Finn and the blade as lantern light danced on the glossy metal. He sheathed the blade and strapped it snug to his waist, where it swayed belt to knee.

"Ay," Red Beard smiled, "a proper fit for ya, Lit'le Finn."

"T'anks Captain," Finn smiled, still trying out his pirate accent.

"Now, for yer naked face," Red Beard said, turning back to the wardrobe.

Finn blushed. He'd never thought of his face as naked before.

The captain quickly fished through several high wooden boxes. Turning, he held a variety of wigs – different styles of beard in different shades of brown.

"Until ye be able to grow yer own, one 'a these 'ill do nicely."

"Ay," Finn replied, nearly drowning in delight.

"Try this on for size," Red Beard smiled, tugging out a thick, scratchy batch of dirty blonde hair, and handing it to Finn.

"Ay," Finn said sliding the beard into place, "It's perfect."

Captain Red Beard helped Finn tighten the beard into place with straps over the ears and around his head.

He smiled, "Now ye be a proper member 'a dis motley crew."

Suddenly, the door swung open a second time.

"Captain," Lucky interrupted, "we're approachin'."

"Raise da banner."

"Ay," Lucky barked, and left the quarters again.

Beyond the door, Finn heard the crew comply as the command echoed between them:

"Raise da banner!" Lucky ordered.

"Banner up!" the crew replied.

"Raise da lantern!" Lucky chanted.

"For the Prince!" the crew replied.

"For the Prince!" Lucky echoed.

Finn listened, and so did Red Beard. With a smile on his face, he whispered the last refrain with his crew and with Lucky, "For the prince."

"For the prince?" Finn asked.

"Ay," Red Beard replied with a hint of sadness, "For the prince."

Then, as the sadness drifted, and excitement for the moment returned, that sparkle came back into the Captain's light blue eyes.

"Now, ya ready for that adventure?" he asked with a wink.

"Ay," Finn replied. Little Finn smiled wide, and gripping the sword with one hand, he stroking his beard with the other.

Red Beard swung the door wide open, and they

rushed out ‑ into stiff wind and dim light atop the Starling.

"WAIT," Sissie interrupted, "You're not really letting him do this are you?"

I started laughing and rolled my eyes.

"Why not?" I asked, just to be obnoxious.

Sissie rolled her eyes at me and looked back at grandpa for an answer.

He just shrugged.

"Grandpa," she continued, "it's not safe! He's way too young to carry a sword, or attack another ship, or steal stuff, or..."

"Grow a beard?" I interrupted her tirade.

This time grandpa started laughing.

"Why are you laughing!" Sissie scolded grandpa, fighting back tears.

"Alright, alright," grandpa chuckled, "settle down Elizabeth."

"But he's so young and it's so dangerous," she insisted.

"Like letting a little girl ride a dragon?" Grandpa asked softly.

Sissie turned her head away, eyes filling with tears,

frustrated and worried.

"That was just a few nights ago, little one," grandpa continued. "Remember?"

"Yes," Sissie whispered, her voice shaking a bit, "but this is different."

"Is it?" Grandpa whispered back.

I started to feel a bit bad about all the teasing.

"Sis," I said, waiting for her to look up, "he'll be okay - he still has us to help him."

Sissie nodded, unconvinced. She kept her eyes down.

"Shall we continue reading?" Grandpa asked.

"Definitely," I replied.

Sissie nodded silently, and grandpa continued to read.

## ❦ 6 ❦

### THE GOVERNOR'S FORTUNE

Finn followed Captain Red Beard to the helm of the Starling. From the helm, Finn could see horizon to horizon. The Starling leaned left as she raced toward a taller, broader boat just a few minutes ahead.

In the crow's nest, Scoop continued to call out directions. Sailors darted left and right across the deck shifting sail lines and preparing ropes. Lucky barked orders with his sword drawn, a long curved blade that shined gold as he waved it, catching bits of lantern light.

The dark sea looked black against a gray horizon line. Above the horizon, dark grey clouds moved swiftly off the starboard side, evidence of the storm earlier that day.

Red Beard leaned into the wheel. The Starling surged toward her foe. Excitement bubbled among the crew. The Starling gained ground.

The Governor's crew had spotted them. He ordered his crew, "Release the sails!"

It was too late. The Starling had a head start and all the momentum, Red Beard's crew was nearly upon them.

Closing in, Little Finn could hear the panicked voices of the opposing crew.

The Starling drew close alongside the governor's ship - her starboard parallel to the Governor's port. The two crews faced each other at sailing speed in mystified silence.

Then, Captain Red Beard shouted boldly into the darkness:

"From light to lantern."

"From light to lantern," his crew echoed.

"From lantern to light."

"From lantern to light," his crew chanted.

Some shipmates hung high on the sail lines, ready to jump. Others held planks, ready to run from one ship to the other.

"Restore the sea, for the Prince!" Red Beard shouted, raising his sword over his head.

"For the prince," the crew cried screamed.

That was the signal. Little Finn watched as his shipmates swarmed the Governor's boat - some leaping into their sails, others crossing planks to the opposing deck.

Captain Red Beard leapt down to the main deck, raced across a plank, and joined the fray.

Little Finn followed.

Pulling his sword from its sheath, Finn charged into the mess of clanging metal, shouts from a panicked crew, and the constant chant from the Red Beard's men:

"For the prince."

GRANDPA PAUSED. Tilting his head back for a moment, he drew in a deep slow breath.

"Grandpa," I prodded, "what is it?"

"Hmm," he hummed, and then whispered something (I couldn't hear what) to himself.

"Grandpa, Finn?" Sissie pushed, "Can we make sure he's still okay?"

"Yes, of course," grandpa smiled.

He continued to read.

FINN JOINED IN THE REFRAIN, swept up in the chaos and excitement. His own sword glistened as it caught bits of light cast by lanterns. The sword held strong when it rattled against opposing blades. He turned and spun forward and back, battling the Governor's crew.

In just a few short moments, the governor's entire crew turned to flee. They scurried like mice into dark spaces below deck. The Starling crew followed, chasing them down and rounding them up. The battle seemed to end nearly before it began. The crew of the Starling cheered, clanging their swords overhead, cheering victory.

Red Beard's men bound the governor's crew by rope, and tied them across the deck. While a few men stood guard, the rest of the Starling crew searched the boat for bounty - taking food, clothing, jewelry, and coin back across the planks to their storehouse below deck.

Most of the governor's crew remained silent as Captain Red Beard and his men emptied their treasure.

Most, but not all.

"You dirty pirates - thieves of the night - emptying our boat to fill your own chests."

The Starling crew ignored him.

"Nothing but dirty pirates!" he shouted again.

But, they continued to ignore his taunts.

"Dirty pirates," he continued, louder, "stealing our treasure in the name of some fairy tale, from days of old."

At this, Lucky turned, swinging his sword wildly, but halting at the throat of the prisoner.

"Our Prince be no fairy tale," Lucky said in a cool and steady tone.

The prisoner's eyes opened wide, as he squirmed away from the blade.

"For the prince," Lucky shouted, pulling back his blade.

"For the prince," the crew echoed.

Without a word from Captain Red Beard, the crew circled the governor's crew on deck. Stepping forward, he spoke:

"Who be the captain 'a dis fine vessel?"

The governor's crew remained silent.

Then, slowly and with great emphasis on every word, Red Beard said, "I'll only be askin' questions once."

The governor's crew began to squirm here and there.

Then, a soft voice in the back spoke up, "The captain wears red."

"Ay," others repeated, "He wears red."

Red Beard nodded, and walking between the bound men, came to one wearing a red band on his arm with the mark of the governor.

"Captain?"

The man looked up, afraid, but didn't speak.

"What be the name of this ship?"

"Fortune," he whispered, afraid and broken.

"Ay," Red Beard nodded.

Then turning to the Fortune's crew, he said: "We be not pirates, but soldiers for the prince."

"For the prince," the crew of the Starling chanted.

"And, until the prince returns," Red Beard continued, with rising volume, "we be the protectors of his sea."

The crew continued chanting, "for the prince."

Calling over the chant, Red Beard continued - his voice rising and sword raised, "Protectors of Bright Water!"

When they heard the name *Bright Water*, the Starling crew erupted in shouts and sword waving. As they returned to the Starling, Finn and Captain Red Beard hung back, still standing over the Fortune's captain.

"Fortune be yer lucky name," Red Beard whispered to the Captain. "I'll be sparin' yer lives, for the sake of the prince."

The captain looked up, startled by this act of mercy. His eyes raised to met Red Beard's.

"Many thanks," he whispered.

At that, Red Beard turned and left the Fortune. Finn followed.

In less than an hour's time, they had tracked, boarded, looted, and left one of the governor's finest ships. Now, they were off. Banner lowered, the Starling peeled left away from Fortune, toward the dark sea and distant shore.

Behind them, the crew remained bound and silent, unsure what to think - the strange pirates, the story of a prince, the Captain's light blue eyes, and the dream of Bright Water.

For some, the mention of *Bright Water* stirred their hearts - a hope, a longing for stories long ago lost at sea. For others, *Bright Water* was nothing but the folly of children, and a guise for piracy.

For the Fortune's captain, Red Beard's mercy would be difficult to forget.

*Perhaps the legends are true*, his mind raced. *Perhaps Bright Water exists after all.*

## ✿ 7 ✿

## LORD EMIGRE'S CITADEL

The Starling moved swiftly, despite the extra load, and her crew celebrated with laughter and dancing as she stole through twilight toward the shore. Red Beard chose a route that chased the storm, so fair winds hurried their escape.

Finn found himself at the helm a second time. Standing next to Red Beard, he started to realize that the adrenaline rush he felt boarding the Fortune had faded.

Now, he replayed each moment in his mind's eye. Giddy excitement mixed with a strange feeling that he was growing up somehow.

The swirl of emotion left him speechless. He stood quiet, watching the Starling rise and dip as she raced ahead.

Captain Red Beard, also stared at the horizon. He seemed to be humming softly under his breath.

Another thought rose up in Finn's mind – a nervous thought. The Fortune's crew had called them pirates – scoundrels and thieves. Also, they had stolen, and they left the crew bound on deck with no supplies.

Finn felt safe with Red Beard, but wondered if he was helping the right side.

On the other hand, something strange had happened when he heard the name *Bright Water*. Like in a dream, the mere name lifted Finn off the ground. The place he imagined – so different from this Dark Sea – ignited a flame deep inside his spirit.

If there was such a place, Finn wanted to go there.

"I FELT the same way when I heard you read it, grandpa," I interrupted.

"Me too," Sissie chimed in.

"Me three," Grandpa smiled.

"Have you been there?" I asked.

"I'm not sure we have time for me to tell you that story," grandpa smiled. "Finn needs us to keep reading right now."

Sissie and I nodded in agreement, and grandpa continued.

AFTER SEVERAL HOURS, Freckles arrived at the helm to take the first night shift. Captain Red Beard led Finn to Lucky, who found Finn an empty hammock in a room with sleeping sailors he'd not yet met.

"We'll be to port in early morning," Lucky said, helping Finn settle into his swinging bed.

"Ay," Finn replied.

"Get some rest Lit'le Finn," Lucky smiled. "Yer adventure be jus' beginnin'."

Finn nodded and settled in. Exhausted, he fell asleep almost instantly.

On deck, Lucky stood beside Freckles at the Helm.

"An' what ya be thinking' of da boy now?" Lucky spoke steady and soft.

Freckles ignored him.

"An' his skill wit da sword?"

Freckles kept staring straight ahead, "What ye be gettin' at?"

"Ya know what I be gettin' at."

"Ay," Freckles whispered, looking straight ahead, "perhaps."

"Ay," Lucky repeated, "perhaps, indeed."

WHEN FINN WOKE, the hammock hung steady. Lifting his head, he noticed empty hammocks. Soft morning light filtered down a stairway beyond the door.

Finn rolled to his side, and suddenly the hammock twisted, promptly dumping him on the hard, wooden floor.

Finn groaned and picked himself up. Then, anxious to not miss any part of the adventure, he adjusted his beard, strapped on his sword, and rushed up the stairway onto the deck.

To his surprise, the Starling rested at dock in a narrow cove. Hills wrapped around the cove in all directions, blocking wind and wave. Beyond the dock, Finn saw a small town.

On deck, the crew busied themselves hauling yesterday's treasure down planks, onto the dock, and into town. He spotted Captain Red Beard near a plank, talking with a well dressed man.

Red Beard waved him over.

"Lord Emigre, this here be Lit'le Finn," Red Beard smiled.

"Pleased to meet you young Finn," Lord Emigre

also smiled. "The captain speaks highly of you."

Finn bowed slightly in thanks.

"And our small citadel thanks you. Your adventure has provided for this community's survival."

"I don't understand," Finn responded.

"I suppose not," Lord Emigre replied. "There is much to tell. Please, come with me."

Red Beard agreed, and the three of them walked off the Starling, down the dock, and into the citadel.

Finn noticed Lucky and Freckles directing the crew as they unloaded the treasure. Lucky offered a wave.

Beyond the dock lush green fields covered the land on either side of the road they walked. The lush land ran right up to a large city wall made of stone, with guards on top. Finn, Red Beard and Emigre followed the cobblestone path beneath an archway in the wall, and into the citadel.

From there, Lord Emigre gave them a tour of the city - introducing Finn to a variety of townspeople throughout the morning and into early afternoon.

It seemed that some of the treasure would be divided up among Lord Emigre's people. The rest was loaded into carts heading to neighboring villages.

"Since the darkness," Lord Emigre had said, "the

governor has taken to cruelty, and the people of the land have suffered."

As dull sunlight faded into dusk's twilight, Red Beard and Little Finn caught up with the rest of the Starling's crew at a large hall built for food and celebration. Finn settled into a wooden table with Captain Red Beard and Lord Emigre.

Large oil lanterns hung like chandeliers down the center of the long hall, and torches along the side walls added to the flickering golden light.

Once everyone had enjoyed their share of food and drink, the crew began to clink their drinks.

Lucky rose from his seat and hollered over the sound of clanging mugs, "It's time fer da tales to be spun Captain."

A loud cheer rose up from around the hall.

"Alright, ye sickly scabbards. Where to begin," the Captain stood and stepped away from the table, like an actor taking the stage.

The crew roared with excited expectation.

"Long ago, in the days of me father's father, this land was not dark."

The crowd interrupted with cheers. Red Beard waved his arms to quiet them, and continued.

"In that day, there be a prince - a mighty prince

who ruled the land with honor. Where he ruled, the wicked fled."

The crowd cheered.

"Where he ruled, the poor were cared for…"

More cheers.

"…and the soldiers had little to do.

And again, a loud cheer roared through the hall.

"While the prince ruled, peace stretched across the sea and land. We must not forget the goodness of our prince!"

Red Beard paused as the crowd cheered. Then, he waved his arms again to quiet them.

Finn leaned forward, just as he did when grandpa read a story. His heart pounded inside his chest with excitement.

"Then," Red Beard went on, "the prince journeyed."

Sadness quieted his voice. "Our prince rules over many lands, and challenges arose far away that demanded his presence."

"When he left, the great peace did not last."

## ❧ 8 ❧

## OUT OF THE PAGES

"Our world began to change."

The crowd booed and grumbled at this, shouting out ill words about the governor. Red Beard waved his arms again to quiet them.

"Ay," he went on, "darkness has come, but we remember the Bright Water!"

The crowd erupted again with cheers, chanting "Bright Water, Bright Water, Bright Water," until Red Beard raised his arms for silence.

"Tonight, I'll tell ye all a story me father's father told me," Red Beard paused to catch Finn's eye, and shot him a wink.

"A long time ago, when the sky be bright and the water be clear as me own eyes, there came a fleet of three dark ships dragging thick clouds behind them.

While they were still a long way off, men of the port spotted the clouds and sent word to the King."

A hush fell across the crowd. They, like Finn, hung on every word as Red Beard unfolded his story in the dancing light of lanterns.

"Upon hearing about the dark clouds, the King smiled. He had been waiting for this moment. He had been warned. The King dressed a royal ship with the banner of Bright Water - a lantern sewn square in the center sail. And sailing the ship himself, with only a small crew of trusted men, he met the dark boats just beyond the shallows."

"Me father's father be on that boat that day," Red Beard went on, "an' he never forgot the faces of the men on those three dark boats, nor the thick clouds, nor the dark water that followed them."

A heavy silence hung over the crowd.

"As the King's boat approached, the admiral of the dark fleet requested permission to land in Bright Water. 'You've no reason to come, and no reason to stay,' the King replied. But the admiral insisted, and as he did, the dark water behind their boats pushed forward, pressing past the King's own. 'You'll do well to respect our land,' the King said in a calm and solemn voice, his confidence unswayed by the spreading darkness."

"The admiral was also unswayed. A hideous laugh escaped his lips, as they separated in a sinister smile. 'Very well,' he said, 'We shall invite ourselves,' and in a flash of red, he disappeared."

Red Beard paused, as goosebumps rose on arms around the room.

"Me father's father remembers well the moments that followed. The admiral disappeared for but a moment. When he reappeared it was on the King's boat."

"Again, the King remained calm. 'We are not afraid of ye or ye darkness,' he said, raising his voice slightly for emphasis. And, raising his voice further as he drew his sword, the King said, 'This is not your land, this is the land of Bright Water!'"

The crowd erupted in raucous cheering. Finn felt his chest swell - with love for this King, for this place, and for the way he imagined the world ought to be.

SUDDENLY, back in the basement, the pages of the book flashed bright. Startled, grandpa leaned back and dropped the book onto the table. Sissie and I jumped back from the table and watched it with wide eyes.

The pages turned rapidly on their own - forward

and back. As they did, bits of light shot up from the page like tiny comets launched into the basement.

Grandpa got to his feet and stepped back from the table. The basement was alive with bright white fireworks. We all watched, amazed at the book's excitement.

After a few moments, an explosion of blinding light burst from the page.

Sissie and I turned away, falling to the basement floor.

Grandpa stood his ground.

After the flash, I heard a loud thump. Blinded by the flash, I squinted, working hard to see again.

As my eyes adjusted, I saw an outline, like a shadow. Our basement had a visitor - someone new had landed on the other side of the table.

Grandpa casually took his seat. I looked at Sissie, still rubbing her eyes to shake the light.

"Dad?" the new voice asked. "What are you doing down here?"

I knew that voice.

"Mom!" I shouted, still blinking.

Sissie and I ran to her.

"What in the world are you two doing here?" she asked, shooting a look full of questions at grandpa as she hugged us.

"Hello dear," grandpa smiled. "I might ask you the same thing."

"I'm not sure I've got time to explain," with another look of concern toward grandpa. "Have you seen Charles?"

"We have!" Sissie said with delight. "We saw father in the last story, helping Charlotte!"

"Charlotte?" Mom asked, sending another look toward grandpa.

"Yeah," I chimed in, "in Egypt."

Mom tilted her head toward grandpa with a look more stern than concerned.

He cracked a smile, "They're quick learners."

Mom shook her head and scanned the room.

"Where's Little Finn?"

Sissie and I looked at grandpa this time. Sitting back, he folded his arms and smiled again.

"Dad?" Mom asked in her mom voice.

"He's with Red Beard."

"Red Beard?" Mom's jaw dropped. "You can't be serious."

"In the citadel with Emigre," grandpa continued.

"No, not the citadel."

"Dear, he's fine," grandpa said softly. "Red Beard's halfway through the story of..."

"It's not fine," mom interrupted.

Sissie and I exchanged glances. Mom liked to worry, but she seemed especially concerned about Finn.

"Dad," she went on, "things are shifting."

*Shifting*, I wondered.

"Shifting how?" grandpa asked.

"Calamitous is inside."

"Impossible," grandpa leaned back from the table in disbelief. "Calamitous?"

"I saw him," mom insisted.

Grandpa's face dropped, "But how? He hasn't visited since..."

"That's not important now. The stakes are high."

"Where is Charles?" grandpa asked.

"I was hoping you knew," mom said, surprised. "You last saw him near the tomb?"

"Yes," grandpa recounted. "Then we heard him land in the basement, and disappear again."

"To where?"

"To join you, I thought." grandpa went on.

"In dark water?"

"It was the only other open book," grandpa replied.

"What about Finn?" I interrupted.

"Right," mom said, turning back to us. "He's at the citadel?"

"Yes, with…"

"Red Beard," Sissie interrupted.

"And Lord Emigre," grandpa finished.

"They aren't safe," mom continued. "The Governor is on the move."

"The governor? But how?" grandpa asked. "Since when?"

Mom stared back. Her face answered his question.

"No," he sighed.

"I'm afraid so," mom sighed.

"Calamitous!" grandpa muttered under his breath.

## 9

## THE GOVERNOR'S GRASP

"**A**s in Master Calamitous?" I asked.

"The same," mom said, turning again to Sissie and I.

"We need to get back to the story," mom continued, as she pulled another chair toward the table. "Finn needs our help."

The book throbbed with white light.

"Where is that scene?" mom mumbled, delicately flipping pages.

"There," grandpa interrupted her search, pointing near the top of the page.

"The governor is on the move," mom spoke directly at the book in a clear, calm voice. "The citadel is in immediate danger."

The book flashed bright.

Leaning back from the book, she smiled at Sissie and I.

"It'll be okay," mom said softly, more to convince herself than us, I think.

Grandpa slid the book toward himself, "Yes, here we are, back in the hall, the middle of Red Beard's story."

He continued to read.

"RAISING his voice further as he drew his sword, the King said, 'This is not your land, this is the land of Bright Water!'"

The crowd erupted in raucous cheering. Finn felt his chest swell - with love for this King, for this place, and for the way he imagined the world ought to be.

As the crowd cheered, Finn noticed a small piece of paper drifting down from the rafters. Red Beard noticed too.

Finn leapt onto his table and grabbed the note. Red Beard walked toward Finn's table. The crowd continued to cheer.

Finn unfolded the note and quickly read it to himself:

*The governor is on the move. The citadel is in danger.*

His eyes grew wide. His jaw tightened. As Red Beard arrived, Finn handed him the note. This was not good news.

Red Beard quickly read the note to himself:

*The governor is on the move. The citadel is in danger.*

The Captain's jaw also tightened. He quickly waved his arms to quiet the crowd.

"Friends of Bright Water," he called out, "we have unsettling news."

But before Red Beard could share the note with his audience, a high pitched whistle interrupted their celebration, followed by the shudder of breaking timber. People across the hall dove left and right to avoid a flaming cannonball as it ripped through the roof and crashed into several tables. The ceiling ignited in flames, casting sparks across the hall.

Terror took hold of those in the hall. Red Beard looked past Finn to Lord Emigre.

"The governor," Red Beard called over the chaos, "he's here."

Emigre, already on his feet, took command of his people.

"To the tunnels!" his voice rose clear and calm above the chaos. "Gather your families. Leave all else."

As he spoke, another whistle warned of a second cannonball. It burst through the other end of the hall, shattering more tables and igniting the wall in flames.

The people heard Lord Emigre and, organizing themselves, hurried to the far end of the hall. Several strong men lifted sections of the floor, revealing stone tunnels hidden beneath the city.

Lord Emigre turned to Red Beard, "Our time to part has come again, old friend."

Red Beard nodded, extending his arm.

"The attack must be from the South," Lord Emigre continued. "They have crested the ridge which means the harbor, and the Starling, should be safe for now. Hurry, and you may escape the Bay before his fleet arrives.

Their firm handshake turned into a hug.

Then, Red Beard stepped away to gather his men.

Finn watched as Emigre directed his people. He was a kind ruler, and a friend of Bright Water. Lucky tugged at Little Finn's coat, and turning, the two of them chased after Red Beard and the crew of the Starling. Finn tried to push away his fear as they followed the Captain. He focused on Lucky. They hurried through a maze of cobbled streets, aiming for the harbor.

Deepening dusk threw long shadows across the city, providing cover for their escape. Behind them, the whistle of cannonballs continued, igniting thatched roofs across the citadel. Each explosion startled the crew as they raced to the dock. Red Beard led the way, steady as ever.

Looking over his shoulder, Finn could see the governor's army atop the southern hills. He could see them pouring down the hillside on horse and foot.

He wondered about the people of the citadel – would the tunnels hold? Would they really be safe?

Red Beard's crew reached the city gates. They moved quickly between shadows all the way to the dock. They untied and boarded the Starling under the stealth of dusk. In the distance, Finn heard soldiers breaching the citadel wall on the southern barrier – war cries and clanging metal.

The air felt stale against Finn's face. Red Beard's crew quickly unfurled the sails, but they hung empty in dead air. The crew pushed out oars to row her out of the cove.

Finn headed to the upper deck for a better view. He looked back as a small wake spread behind the Starling, marking the space between their escape and the dock. Finn watched in horror as dark smoke rose from the now burning citadel. Fire-lit arrows danced in the sky like fireflies finding their way into the city, igniting homes and shops.

Finn could see dark outlines pouring into the citadel. The Governor's army, scaling the wall like rats. He thought about Lord Emigre and the townspeople, driven out of their homes - into the ground. Anxious, he closed his eyes and took a deep breath.

Then, he thought of the warning, his note. He thought of those watching over him. Finn felt safe. He remembered the courage of the King. His heart swelled again. Finn lifted his eyes back to the citadel. He would need some courage of his own in this adventure.

The crew paddled hard, pushing beyond the center of the cove. In a moment, they would turn beyond the point and stretch into open water.

Suddenly Scoop called down from the crow's nest, "Arm yerselfs, there be villains in the dark waters ahead!"

"To arms," Lucky echoed from the bow.

"Ay!" Captain Red Beard called from the helm. "To arms, men, we be fightin' for the prince."

"For the Prince," the crew echoed.

Finn looked away from the burning citadel. The

Starling began turning North, through the mouth of the cove. That's when Finn saw it. Six tall ships waiting for them just outside the Lord Emigre's harbor.

Little Finn's heart dropped. Terror replaced the swell of courage he mustered. Eyes wide, he froze along the side of the ship.

With banners raised and cannons loaded, the governor's fleet waited for the Starling in the deep, dark water.

Red Beard called out to his crew, "Oars in, cannons out boys," prepare yer'selves for battle.

Finn tried to breath. They couldn't possibly win.

His heart raced. The governor's fleet dwarfed the Starling - tall ships, each much bigger than Red Beard's vessel.

All six ships flew the black tower flag.

"Lit'le Finn," Lucky called up from the main deck, "We're not lost yet, mate - grab a sword."

Following Lucky's order, Little Finn hustled below deck to arm himself.

*Breathe,* Little Finn thought, *just breathe. This is your adventure - for the prince.* Inside his heart, courage wrestled fear.

Skipping stairs, Finn raced to the deck, sword strapped to his side, Finn passed the main royale and climbed netting between the starboard rail and center deck. He turned to face the enemy. Scanning the horizon, he counted three boats on either side of the Starling. Sailors loyal to the Governor lined the rails of each boat, armed with sword and shield.

The governor commanded a mighty fleet.

Like a bird in the hand, the Starling had no where to fly. The Captain and his men were surrounded.

Red Beard's crew had obeyed their orders. The oars were in, and cannons stood ready to fire. Trapped or not, Captain Red Beard and his salty crew would not surrender without a fight.

Beyond the harbor, a light northerly breeze rippled across the deck, nudging the Starling toward her enemy.

Scanning the scene, Finn spotted a tall, devilish figure in a dark cloak. He stood firm in the bow of the second ship, beside a short man dressed in black armor and wearing a crown.

"Dad, stop, before it's too late," mom interrupted grandpa's reading.

## 10

## A DEVILISH FIGURE

"What's going on?" I asked.

"Is that guy like Lark?" Sissie added.

Grandpa leaned back from the book, "It's really him?" he muttered.

"Yes," mom answered.

"Who?" I interrupted again.

"Calamitous," they whispered in unison.

"We've got to get Finn out of there!" Sissie exclaimed.

Mom and grandpa glanced at Sissie, and then back at each other.

I leaned back in the chair, and watched. Mom looked pretty freaked out and grandpa still seemed surprised. I thought of Lark and Devlin. They seemed terrified whenever they mentioned Calamitous.

If *they* were that scared, this couldn't be good.

After a lengthy pause, grandpa leaned forward.

"It may not be safe to pull Finn out," he whispered. "We... we may be too late."

Mom nodded in agreement.

I shot a glance at Sissie. Her eyes were welling up with tears. I was scared too.

Grandpa continued to read.

"FANCIES HIMSELF A KING," Freckles called up to Finn. "That crowned man be the governor."

Finn kept his eyes fixed ahead, on the man in the dark cloak.

The governor stepped forward and raised his sword.

"Captain of the Scally-wags," he called out to Red Beard, "surrender now, and we *might* let your despicable crew live, after we sink your pathetic boat."

"Strong words," Freckles whispered up to Finn, "for a cowardly governor."

The crew turned to watch Red Beard respond. He stood firm atop the stern, behind the wheel.

Finn listened, but kept his eyes on the devilish figure in the black cloak.

"You see our flag. You see the lantern," Red Beard called back, in a strong and steady voice. "We sail under a different banner. We follow the rule of the Prince. We will not surrender."

As Red Beard spoke, Finn watched the man in the dark cloak whisper to the governor.

"Are you too proud to see that you've already lost?" the governor taunted.

"Avast," Red Beard replied, "do not mistake me confidence for pride." Then, raising his sword, he cried out, "for the Prince!"

The crew echoed the call, "for the Prince!"

As they did, Finn saw the governor nod toward the devilish figure. Suddenly, in a flash of red light, the man in the dark cloak disappeared.

Finn grinned, suddenly remembering. The crew continued to chant.

*Of course*, Finn thought to himself.

Dropping to the ship deck, Finn looked up to the helm. Then it happened just as he expected - a second flash. A swirl of red light, and the man in the dark cloak appeared, right beside Captain Red Beard.

Red Beard swung around to face the flash of red - the devilish figure.

"You are a fool," the devilish figure muttered, and drawing a dagger from his dark cloak, he plunged it into Red Beard's side.

"No!" Finn cried out from the deck. Freckles and Lucky saw it too.

Red Beard fell forward, into the arms of the man who stabbed him.

"To the helm," Freckles hollered, as he and several mates raced forward to save their captain.

Concentrating, Finn imagined himself on the helm. In a swirl of white light, he disappeared. In a second flash, he appeared on the helm, directly behind the devilish figure.

The man in the cloak noticed the flash of light. So did Red Beard.

Finn knelt, and Red Beard mustered his remaining strength to shove the devilish figure toward Finn. The man in the cloak fell backward, tripping over Little Finn's crouched body. Before landing on the deck, the devilish figure disappeared in another swirl of red light.

Finn gathered himself and hurried toward the captain. The whole crew rushed toward the helm. But there was no time. Instantly, the man in the cloak reappeared - another swirl of red light.

"More white light?" the devilish figure laughed,

mocking Finn with his raspy, tired voice. "How amusing."

In a single terrifying motion, he picked up Little Finn and hurled him into the dark water. Then, the man in the dark cloak turned back to Red Beard. Behind him, Finn landed with a splash.

"WE CAN'T JUST KEEP READING like this!" I interrupted, my eyes welling up with tears. "Finn's drowning and the Captain's dying! We have to do something!"

Sissie's rubbed tears from her eyes. She wanted to speak, but couldn't find the right words.

"Grandpa?" I continued. "Mom?"

"It's not that simple, Riles," Mom turned to me with a soft voice. "Calamitous is breaking the rules, doing more than he ought to change the story."

"The rules?" Sissie whispered.

"Look at the book," mom pointed.

It continued to pulse with a soft white light.

"Do you see the binding?" she continued.

It looked worn, looser then before. Several pages had tugged free.

"There are limits, children," grandpa added.

"Limits to how we help heroes of each story - limits to how we shape events."

"When we go past those limits," mom continued, "the story becomes fragile - unstable."

"That means we should really get Finn out, right?" Sissie asked, regaining her voice.

"No, sweetheart," mom said softly, "It's not safe for him to flash home."

"Ever?" I asked, tears falling down my cheek.

Silence.

I looked at grandpa, and saw tears behind his own glasses.

"Things are more difficult than I expected, Riles," grandpa spoke just above a whisper. "We must hope Finn and your Father can find a way to make things better."

Mom turned to grandpa.

"Dad," she urged, "best to keep reading?"

"Yes, dear," grandpa sighed, turning back to the glowing pages.

THE CREW RACED to the helm. Lucky ran to the rail, hoping to spot Little Finn. Freckles and several others drew swords as they approached the devilish figure.

Red Beard looked pale - one arm holding his bleeding side, the other leaning heavily on the wheel, his blue eyes still glowing bright.

"We will never surrender," he sputtered at the man in the dark cloak. "We fight for Bright Water - for the Prince!"

The devilish figure laughed, and seeing the crew with swords drawn, he disappeared in a swirl of red light.

Red Beard collapsed into Freckles' arms.

Once the man in the dark cloak disappeared, the battle began in earnest. With a raise of his hand, the governor ordered the attack. Explosions sent cannonballs hurling toward the Starling. Sailors from the two closest boats used mast lines to swing from their deck to the Starling. Swords shined in the dusk and firelight, and the Starling's crew spread to protect her from onslaught.

Freckles lifted Red Beard and rushed him to the Captain's quarters, sending another sailor to summon the ship's medic. Red Beard's deep wound bled badly. Freckles feared the worst.

Along the rail, Lucky continued scanning for the body of Little Finn, ready to jump at the first sign of life.

Dim, several feet below the surface, he saw a flash

of white light. He grinned. Then, he saw a second flash of white. As bad as things seemed, Lucky grinned again.

Two flashes of white light could only mean good news.

## ❧ 11 ❧

## FULL SAILS

Finn gasped for air.

*Where am I*, he wondered. Soaked, he blinked as his eyes adjusted to the dark, musty space.

"Finn," the voice felt familiar.

The room rocked slightly left and right. Finn could feel the sticky salt of dark water dripping off his limbs and trickling down his nose.

*The Starling*, he thought. *Dark Water*.

Sitting up, he wiped his bearded face and tried to remember the last few moments.

"Finn, are you all right?"

The outline of a familiar man hung over him. The arms reached out to hug him close.

"Father?"

"Thank God, you're alive."

"CHARLES!" Grandpa leaned back from the book with a wide smile.

Mom wiped back the water welling in her eyes. She turned toward Sissie and me with the same smile.

I wanted to speak, but the words got stuck in my throat like a twisted lump.

"That's good, right?" Sissie asked.

Mom nodded, still fighting back tears and smiling.

Grandpa nodded too, and leaning forward, continued to read.

FINN COUGHED, spitting up salty water. His head spun a bit. He leaned into his father's hug.

"What are you doing here?" Finn asked.

"Same as you," father whispered.

"What am I doing here?" Finn continued.

"We fight for Bright Water," father whispered, "for the Prince."

Finn smiled.

"You gave me quite a scare," father continued,

"standing up to Calamitous like that took real guts – real courage."

"Calamitous?"

"The man in the cloak?" father went on. "The red flash?"

Finn started to remember – the helm, Red Beard, the devilish figure.

"I flashed!" Finn smiled.

"I saw," father whispered back.

Finn paused, remembering the rest. Father waited. Overhead, muffled shouting and distant explosions interrupted the quiet rock of the boat.

"Did we escape?"

"No."

"Is Red Beard," Finn's throat tightened as he imag- ined the worst, "is he okay?"

"No."

"Father," Finn looked, "I feel scared."

"Me too."

"Can we just go home?"

"It's not that simple," father replied. "Is that what you want?"

"No."

Father smiled, "I didn't think so."

"Why in the world would Finn want to stay?" I interrupted.

"He's starting to believe," mom whispered.

Grandpa nodded.

"I don't understand," Sissie said.

I didn't either.

"You will," grandpa smiled lightly, "you will."

Then, he continued to read.

"What do we do?" Finn asked.

"You know what to do."

"for Bright Water?" Finn smiled.

"for the Prince," Father whispered back.

Then, father hugged Finn and disappeared in a flash of white.

Finn felt his arms fall as father slipped away.

*Well*, Finn thought, *here goes nothing*.

In a flash of white, the dark musty room was empty.

With a second flash, Finn found himself in the captain's quarters.

"Lit'le Finn!" Red Beard said with a cough and grimace.

Outside, the shouts and explosions sounded much closer.

"We're still in the middle of it all?" Finn asked, surprised.

"Ay Lit'le one," Freckles muttered. "And it's not lookin' good for our side."

Lucky burst into the captain's quarters.

"What?" he froze, "You're here?"

"Ay!" Finn replied with a smile.

"You were the flash?"

"Ay!"

Lucky ran over and wrapped Lit'le Finn in a warm hug.

"Gave me quite a scare there, matey!"

"Enough yackin'," Freckles interrupted, "We're losing the Captain here, and in a few more minutes the Starling 'ill be underwater."

"Ay," Lucky replied. "What do ya have in mind, friend?"

"Fight to the end," Red Beard muttered from the bed.

"Not this time," Freckles said to Red Beard. Then, turning to Lucky he whispered, "We loose the sails and pray for wind. We've got to get our Captain to Bright Water."

GRANDPA LIFTED his eyes from the page and gave mom a strange look. She nodded in agreement.

"What?" Sissie and I asked, feeling a bit left out.

"I think we can help them," grandpa replied.

The book flickered.

"But how?" I asked, exasperated. "A clue's not going to help. They need a doctor and some wind – and quick."

"Exactly," mom smiled.

"Really?" Sissie said, starting to smile. "We can do that?"

The book flickered bright again.

"Do what?" I asked, feeling totally lost.

Sissie smiled at me, then turning to the book said:

"Strong winds, carry them to Bright Water!"

The book seemed to pulse with bubbling white light.

"Huh," I said leaning back with a smile. "Great idea, Sis!"

"Shall we?" mom asked grandpa.

Grandpa shot me a wink, and continued reading.

"AY, MATEY," Lucky answered, "that's the spirit. You two go, I'll keep an eye on Red Beard."

As Lucky spoke, the boat lurched sideways – another explosion on deck, another canon ball ripping through the Starling.

Freckles and Finn nearly tumbled forward and drew their swords. Red Beard groaned.

"I don't know how many more hits she can weather before we take on water," Freckles steadied himself.

"Go, be quick," Lucky answered.

Freckles nodded and swinging the door open, he shouted, "Loose the sails."

As he shouted, he felt a rising breeze tickle the stale air.

Finn scrambled out the door behind Freckles and raced up the center mast. He too, could felt the stale, warm breeze starting to move. Halfway to the crow's nest, Finn turned back toward the citadel. He could see the smoke shifting direction, blowing out to sea.

On either side of the citadel, forest trees rustled, and began to lean toward the open sea. A strong wind swept through the leaves. Soon that wind would greet the Starling.

Racing to the helm, Freckles called out a second time, "Loose the sails, and quick!"

"Ay captain," the crew called back, tugging lines

and releasing the sails. They could feel what Finn could see.

As the sails rose, they caught the sudden gusts racing through the forest and across the citadel. One by one, each sail tugged open. Each snapped tight, full of wind.

The Starling heaved forward. The crew cheered as they continued to fight the governor's men across the deck.

"Fire!" the governor cried out in desperatation. "Fire again! Quickly!"

As gusting wind filled her sails, the Starling surged forward, gaining speed and pushing past the governor's fleet. Finn, now sat with Scoop in the crow's nest. They peered down at the scene together, watching the Starling somehow slip past the Governor's powerful fleet of six tall ships.

Fighting continued on the Starling deck. The Governor's men against the Starling crew – until the governor's men realized what was happening.

Realizing the Starling might escape, the Governor's men began jumping overboard – swimming back to their ships.

Red Beard's crew cheered louder as the governor watched in horror.

The Starling continued to pick up speed.

"DID YOU SEE THAT?" I interrupted again.

"What? Sissie followed.

"The book."

"You're right," mom added.

"What?" Sissie asked again.

"It keeps flashing," I went on, "and the pages look tighter."

"The book is healing," mom smiled. "Keep reading."

## 12

### INTO THE FOG

"Attack!" the governor cried out, watching his advantage slip away.

His army obeyed, but the Starling moved swiftly in the fresh wind. Cannonballs meant for Red Beard's crew missed. As the Starling moved forward, the cannonballs passed by, crashing into the Governor's ships on the other side.

"Hold!" the governor cried out, realizing his mistake too late, "Cease fire!"

Beside him, the devilish figure grew angry. Freckles and Little Finn watched in amazement. What seemed like an impossible situation, now looked like a possible victory. The crew of the Starling cheered as the governor nearly sank his own fleet.

"You fool," Master Calamitous bellowed at the Governor. "You're letting them escape."

Cowering at the voice of the man in the dark cloak, the Governor ordered his fleet to turn and chase the Starling. His powerful boats were heavy - slow to turn, and slow to pick up speed.

Meanwhile, the Starling raced toward the horizon, taking full advantage of her lead. Lucky went to check on the Captain, and Freckles manned the helm.

The sun, hidden well below the horizon, still reflected bits of pink and orange against the darkening, deep blue sky. Here and there, stars spied on the Starling as she raced into the open sea.

The crew swelled, energized by their narrow escape. Freckles stood tall at the helm, standing in for the Captain. He guided the ship through mountains of water, swept up by the gusting wind. The rhythmic bob of the bow was a far cry from the chopping rock of stormy seas.

Finn climbed down from the crow's nest and raced to the bow. He yearned to feel the wind at his face. Little Finn's spirit soared as the Starling chased the horizon. His courage rose even as night took hold.

"Ahoy," Scoop hollered down from the crow's nest. Finn stepped away from the bow and looked back across the boat. He could barely see the governor's fleet - a distant silhouette nearly invisible between the sea and sky.

The Governor's fleet continued to chase. In the open sea, they had reached full speed. His tall ships were fast.

Finn felt a nervous pit growing in his stomach.

"Steady on," Freckles hollered from the helm, guiding the Starling and her crew.

Finn headed to the helm for a closer view. Freckles was happy to have the company, though he didn't show it.

"Ya a'right lad?" he asked, in low tone.

"Ay," Finn replied.

"Good."

"They're chasing?"

"Ay," Freckles replied, still looking straight ahead, "no need to worry 'bout them."

"No?"

"No," Freckles solemnly replied. "We weren't saved in the harbor to be sunk in the sea."

Finn smiled behind the beard. Remembering their escape comforted him, somehow, even with the governor chasing.

"We can't outrun them forever, can we?" Finn asked.

"No, we can't," Freckles replied. "We've got to get Red Beard home."

"Home?"

"Ay. Home." Freckles' said quietly, his eyes holding steady to the horizon ahead. "How be da Captain, anyway?"

"I'll see," Finn replied.

Freckles nodded in approval, and Little Finn head down to the captain's quarters. Watching from the starboard rail, Lucky swung onto the deck and followed him into Red Beard's cabin.

"Quite an adventure, ay?" Lucky asked with his usual smile.

"Ay," Finn replied, nervous to see the wounded captain.

They stepped quietly through the door and into the small room. Opposite Red Beard's carved, heavy, wooden desk, was an equally beautiful wooden bed. The medic stood as they entered, and stepped away from the Captain.

"He's stable, for now," he whispered, passing by Lucky and Finn and stepping out onto the deck.

Lucky and Little Finn stepped close on either side of the bed. Red Beard groaned. Turning toward Finn, he smiled a bit and his eyes sparkled.

"Ye saved me life lit'l one."

"Ay," Finn replied, lowering his head.

"That took," Red Beard paused to cough and draw a clean breath, "real courage."

Finn felt the gratitude rush over him. Who was he to help the Captain? But, he had. He laid his hand on the Captain's hand.

"For the prince," Finn whispered.

"Ay, for the prince," Lucky and Red Beard repeated.

Just then, another cry rang out from the crow's nest:"Ahead." A moment later the whole crew cheered.

"What's happening?" Finn whispered to Lucky.

The captain smiled again, and through a cough he whispered, "Home."

Finn looked to Lucky, who was nodding.

"HOME?" I interrupted. "What's he talking about?"

Grandpa leaned back from the book with a smile.

"Still can't wait to hear it in the story?"

Sissie jumped in, "Are you kidding me? Finn and dad are in there. We can't get them out, and Calamitous is ruining the book. Now you're telling us the governor's fleet is closing in and Starling's crew is cheering?"

"Red Beard must know something you don't," mom said with a smile.

"So, just to be clear," I chimed in again, "you two aren't scared anymore?"

"Let's just say things are looking up," grandpa smiled. "Can I keep reading now?"

Sissie and I nodded, and grandpa continued.

THE MEDIC STEPPED BACK in to tend to the Captain.

"Come on," Lucky said, tugging Finn away.

Back on deck, they headed to the bow.

"There," Lucky said, tugging Finn forward and pointing to the horizon, "Do you see it?"

Finn squinted in the deepening darkness. They stood at the bow, wind sweeping across their faces.

"There," Lucky repeated with growing excitement.

Finn tried to make his eyes see. Left to right, the horizon spread - a clear line between the dark water and the deep blue night sky speckled with stars. Only half the moon helped light the Starboard waters. Finn traced the horizon again with his eyes - a clear line everywhere. Everywhere but...

"There?" Finn asked. "Where the horizon blurs?"

"Ay," Lucky smiled. "That be the fog."

"The fog?"

"Ay," Lucky repeated, "Our last patch of hope lies beneath that fog. Therein lies our home."

As they spoke, Finn noticed the wind had weakened. He looked to the stern. No longer just a silhouette against the horizon, the half moon light revealed four tall ships closing in on the flighty Starling.

"Will we make it?" Finn wondered aloud.

Ahead, the blur grew steadily larger. Behind them, the ships drew steadily closer. All the while, the wind slowed.

"Gather the oars, raise the lantern," Freckles hollered from the helm. "Not in the clear yet mates, hold tight through the end."

At Freckles' command, the crew bolted into action. Many headed below deck, pushing oars into the sea and starting to row. Several carried oars back to the deck and headed to the bow.

Lucky raced below deck and emerged with a large black lantern, much like the one on the Starling's flag. He carried it past the crew at the bow and hooked the lantern to a tie on rope connected to the bowsprit - a carved wooden pole that stretched in front of the bow like a narwhal's horn.

Lucky pulled the rope through a pulley system and tugged until the lantern reached the tip of the bowsprit, casting light into the fog ahead of the Starling.

Off the stern, the Governor's fleet approached. They were nearly close enough to fire.

The wind continued to fade, and sails on the Starling fell empty.

She glided forward on whatever momentum she had left.

The wind had faded to near stillness.

"Won't they chase us into the fog?" Finn looked to Lucky for an answer.

"No, lad," he replied, eyes scanning the waters ahead, "far too dangerous."

"Dangerous?"

"Ay, look."

Finn peered ahead, beyond the gently swaying lantern, passed the tip of the bowsprit.

Craggy rocks guarded the bank of fog.

Over his shoulder, Finn heard the governor commanding his men:

"Fire! Fire at will."

An explosion of fireworks sent cannonballs hurtling into the night. The Starling's crew braced for the worst. The first two shots missed starboard with loud splashes.

*Nearly there*, Finn thought, keeping his eyes steadily

fixed on the water ahead. As he did, Finn noticed a change in the water. The darkness thinned.

Beneath, there was light - not the silver reflection of the half moon, but a softer blue light. Lucky saw Finn staring into the depths.

"Ay, ye see it?"

Finn nodded, still staring off the bow.

"What you see is all that remains. All that is left of the bright water," Lucky sighed. "At last, we be almost home."

## 13

### BRIGHT WATER

Once inside the fog, the crew heard little from the governor or his fleet. Loud commands and exploding cannons couldn't break the eerie silence that surrounded them inside the fog.

Command of the vessel now fell to Lucky. Hanging over the bow, he guided them through the rocky crags.

Lucky called out directions to Freckles, who continued to steer from the helm. Two mates on either side of the bow used oars to shove the Starling back to center, carefully navigating rock outcroppings to the left and right.

Lucky knew the waters well. He'd been here many times before. Neither the night nor the fog could fool him.

The oarsmen below deck kept the Starling moving forward, one stroke at a time. All the while, the glow of soft blue light continued to grow.

With Lucky, Freckles, and the rest of the crew occupied, Finn headed to the Captain's quarters. As he stepped in, the medic shifted seats.

"A bit of air?" Red Beard mumbled.

The medic propped the door open, and sat back down. Finn sat next to the Captain. Red Beard looked weak. Finn tried to be brave.

"I can feel it," Red Beard mumbled. "The fog be heavy."

"Ay," Finn spoke, uncomfortably looking down at his own hands.

The captain coughed. Outside, they could hear Lucky calling out directions as the soft tug of oars pulled the Starling forward.

"How's the water," Red Beard mumbled, grabbing Finn's arm tight, "How's the look of it?"

"Beautiful Captain," Finn replied, looking up. "I've never seen anything like it."

"Ay," he replied, with a fresh sparkle in his eyes. "Beautiful indeed. Imagine water like that spread across the whole sea."

"Ay," Finn replied, now locked on Red Beard's bright blue eyes.

"In the day of the Prince..." the Captain's voice broke off into a violent cough.

Finn looked away. He couldn't bear to see the Captain in this much pain. Red Beard cleared his throat, and wiped his mouth with his free hand.

"It's alright, lit'l Finn," Red Beard spoke in a muffled whisper.

Finn felt his eyes swell with tears. It wasn't alright.

Then, Scoop called from the crow's nest: Land ahoy! Signal the citadel!"

Finn stood, eyeing the door.

"Go," the Captain mumbled, "tell me what you see."

"Ay!"

Finn stepped toward the door. Fog still shrouded the Starling.

"The crew is raising a flag alongside the lantern," Finn relayed. "A triangle, checkered red and white."

"Ay," Red Beard smiled, closing his eyes a bit.

"Wait, the fog is thinning," Finn went on. "There, beyond the fog, I see an island, and a hill covered in lights."

"Ay, home."

As the Starling emerged from the fog, Finn saw it. A magnificent city surrounded by a strong wall.

In front of the wall sat two large boulders, and

from the boulders, a winding path stretched toward the sea, where it met a simple dock.

"It looks magnificent and strong," Finn whispered.

Indeed," Red Beard replied. "Dat be the Prince's home, the city on a hill, the Citadel of Bright Water. We'll not be called pirates here."

Suddenly, the air erupted with bugling.

"Why are they bugling?"

"For me," the Captain coughed, and then smiled. "The checkered flag is our cry for help, and the be answering."

It only took a few moments for the Starling to cross the remaining sea and settle at the dock. Lucky and Freckles raced into the Captain's quarters while the rest of the crew secured the ship.

In those few moments, the citadel had come to life. Wagons and carriages hurried to the dock.

Gently, Freckles lifted Red Beard, and carried him to the gangway. Medics met him there, and helped move the Captain to a carriage. Once they loaded Red Beard, the carriage raced up the winding path and into the city.

As the carriage stole away, with the Captain, Finn noticed a well dressed man standing back from the crowd and watching. He had a thick dark beard and a warm smile.

Lucky stepped off the dock, and directed the crew. Townsfolk joined the crew, unloading cargo and examining the Starling for damage.

The Starling took a beating in the battle outside Lord Emigre's citadel. The race toward Bright Water also took a toll.

All around him, Finn heard the story recounted over and over by different members of the crew. A buzz swept through the merchants and soldiers listening, excited by the tale of Red Beard's narrow escape, and captivated by the story of the devilish figure.

When all the goods were unloaded, a stream of carts headed up to hill to the city walls. The winding path came alive with laughter, storytelling, and a string of bobbing lanterns.

After organizing the crew, Lucky stepped away from the Starling and headed toward the well dressed man. They shared a warm embrace and quickly fell into conversation.

After a few minutes alone, Little Finn joined Lucky. As he approached, the well dressed man extended his hand for a hearty shake.

"Hiya," he smiled. Ye must Little Finn," he smiled. "Lucky tells me ye had a lot to do wit' this here escape. Well done lad, well done."

"T'anks, sir," Finn replied, looking down a bit, embarrassed by the attention.

"I'm Liam," he went on, "the Steward here until the Prince returns."

Finn nodded.

"Welcome to the Bright Water Citadel. You've each had a long day. Shall we stroll up to the city?"

"Ay," Lucky and Finn replied.

Steward Liam spun on his heels, headed up the dock, and onto the winding path. Lucky walked beside Liam. Finn followed a step behind. They quickly fell back into conversation.

Like the others from the citadel, Steward Liam wanted to hear all about the ambush at Lord Emigre's citadel, the crew's escape to the harbor, the surprise attack from the Governor, the miraculous wind, and their escape across the sea.

Liam seemed particularly interested in the devilish figure who flashed in red.

Finn half listened. His feet kept pace while his mind wandered. Finn turned his eyes toward the sea.

The dock stood out against the soft glow of bright water lit the space between land and fog. The thick fog hung between the sea and sky a good distance off shore – maybe a mile, maybe two. It rose far above the horizon and wrapped around the island in both directions.

As they walked up the steep path, Finn kept thinking that at some point he'd be able to see over the fog - to see the Governor's ship far below, beyond the fog in the dark waters.

That moment never came. No matter how high they walked up the path, the dark water and the Governor's ships remained hidden beyond the fog. Only the bright blue water and starry night sky could be seen.

When they reached the top of the hill, Liam led Lucky and Finn through a narrow pass - between two giant boulders that seemed to guard the city. Beyond the pass, the wall rose up before them. Lucky and Liam paused for a moment.

"Finn, you look weary" the Steward said with a smile. "A bit of sleep will do you well. Shall we find you a place to rest your head?"

Finn nodded. Liam waved to a soldier near the citadel's entrance.

"Find a comfortable bed for Master Finn to pass the night."

The soldier nodded, "Follow me, Master Finn."

Finn took a few steps, and then turned back toward Liam and Lucky.

"What about the Captain?"

Lucky smiled.

"We'll know more in the morning," he said solemnly. "You can see him then."

"Ay," Finn said, and then to Liam, "T'anks for ye hospitality."

"It be me honor, lad."

And with that, Finn followed the soldier, found a bed, and fell fast asleep.

## ❧ 14 ❧

### THE PRINCE'S CITADEL

Little Finn woke to a knock a his door. Groggy, he lifted his head from a comfortable bed in an unfamiliar, dark room.

Another rap at the door.

"Lit'le Finn?"

It sounded like Lucky.

"Ay," he moaned from the bed. "Come in."

Lucky burst through the door with a wide smile and refreshed enthusiasm in his step. Daylight flooded the doorway and Finn covered his face in blankets.

"Can't sleep da whole day away laddie!" Lucky nearly sang, as he danced to the window and drew back long tapestries.

Finn groaned.

"Take a peek, lad," Finn went on, "You've got da best view o'da sea."

Finn slid the blankets off his now-adjusting eyes, and looked toward the window. Thick tapestries framed either side of large opening in the stone wall. His room towered above the city wall, revealing the bright blue sea.

Finn could see the path they had walked last night disappear between the two boulders. It appeared again at the bottom of the hill by the dock. He could also see the harbor. Even in the daylight, it glowed bright blue and stretched to the fog.

The fog rose from the bright water to the blue, cloudless sky.

"Magnificent!" Finn exclaimed.

"Get up," Lucky urged. "It's nearly noon and you've not seen the Capt'n."

Finn jumped out of the sheets, still fully dressed from the night before.

"He's alright then?" Finn smiled, heading for the door.

"Ay," Lucky replied, following. "He will be."

GRANDPA SLID his glasses to his forehead and leaned back from the book.

"It seems things are returning to normal," he smiled. "Great work Sissie."

"It was mom's idea," Sissie giggled, happy to get the praise.

"So are they safe now?" I asked. "Can we pull dad and Finn out of the book and be done with this adventure?"

"Is that what you want?" Grandpa asked, leaning toward me a bit.

"I want them to come home safely," I replied.

"What if their work isn't done?" Mom jumped in. "What if *they* aren't ready?"

"What do you mean?" Sissie asked.

I leaned back, and thinking aloud said, "Is that what you meant about Finn was starting to believe?"

Mom paused, letting me answer my own question.

"But, believe in what?" Sissie pushed.

"What indeed," mom leaned back in her chair with a smile. "The books of course."

Sissie and I exchanged glances.

"The important question is why," grandpa went on. "Why do you think we've been reading these stories?"

"So, you're saying Finn and dad aren't stuck, but

they want to stay inside the story because they have a job to do?"

"Sissie, Riles," grandpa laughed again. "I'm surprised. What *have* you learned this week?"

Then, grandpa stood up from the table. "I'm long overdue for a fresh spot o'tea. Is anyone else thirsty?"

Mom, Sissie, and I all raised our hands, and Grandpa headed up the basements steps.

"Thanks dad," mom called after him.

"Thanks grandpa," Sissie and I hollered.

"So," mom smiled at us, "You've been doing lots of reading this visit, huh?"

We nodded, and dove into a quick retelling of our adventures. I told her all about Drift and my escape from the back of the van inside Captain Kēto's spaceship. We told her about Razo and Winthrop, and I showed her my scar. Sissie shared her adventures with Vilgor, and her time with Charlotte.

As we talked, mom added bits and pieces to our stories. She knew them all - though some of the finer details seemed slightly different. She knew the Lady of the Western Wood well, but had never ridden on Vilgor's back. Mom also knew Drift and Charlotte, but had never met Lark or Layla.

Soon, grandpa returned with two cups of tea and two hot chocolates.

"Catching you up, are they?" grandpa asked mom as he handed out the drinks.

"Indeed," mom said with a smile, "It sounds like we've *all* had quite a week of adventures. I suppose I'm glad you've each had a chance to explore this world of Story Keeping. You're certainly farther along than I was at either of your ages."

She paused before adding, "I'm sure that will come in handy. We may have more stories to visit in the days to come."

She glanced toward grandpa, and he offered a knowing nod.

"Now that I've got my tea," he asked, "shall we get back to Finn's adventure?"

"Yes," we all chimed.

Grandpa picked up his glasses, set them on his nose, and leaned toward the book. The pages flickered a bit.

"Ah yes," he smiled. "Here we are."

LUCKY AND FINN hurried from Finn's turret bedroom, down a staircase, through a courtyard, across the castle, into another turret, and up to the bedroom that held Captain Red Beard.

A dozen people gathered at the door. Lucky pushed his way through the crowd and Finn followed. When Red Beard saw them, he called them both to his bedside.

"Sleeping the day away I see," Lucky chided the Captain.

"Ay," he chuckled and then groaned from the pain of laughing. "I see no reason to rise since our Starling is not yet fixed and full."

Lucky laughed, and the two embraced for a light hug. Again Red Beard groaned.

"And you," he said turning toward Little Finn, "that devilish man would have finished me off had it not been for you and your white light."

As he said "white light," the crowd at the door began whispering.

*The rumors were true? Red Beard had been saved by a newcomer?*

That message quickly spread from the room to the castle, and from the castle to the city.

*White light had returned to Bright Water.*

"What'd I tell ye Freckles," the Captain smiled toward the other side of the bed, "the sea be bringin' us hope after all."

"Ay," Freckles smiled, nodding toward Lucky and Finn. "Hope indeed."

Finn and Lucky fell into quick conversation with Red Beard and Freckles. They recounted the adventure - from the ambush at Lord Emigre's Citadel to their arrival at Bright Water.

"Lads, mark me words. Someday they'll write songs about these adventures," Red Beard smiled.

"Indeed," came a voice from the door, "someday. But this day, you'll be eating your soup and gathering strength.

Liam the Steward entered, followed by a string of castle servants with lunch for Freckles and Red Beard.

Lucky and Finn said goodbye with light hugs and hearty handshakes, and headed for the door. As they did, Liam followed.

"It appears we have some time," Liam asked Lucky. "Shall we show the lad the city?"

Finn nodded yes, and the three of them set off to explore Bright Water Citadel. One afternoon exploring the city quickly turned into several days. For Finn, it was all a blur.

Red Beard's recovery took time. Between visits to see the Captain, Lucky and Finn met with soldiers, statesmen, merchants, and farmers.

Finn heard many stories of the old days, when the Bright Water stretched across the whole sea; before the fog. Those stories warmed his heart and filled his soul. Whenever a story mentioned the prince, his chest would swell with yearning. Finn deeply wanted to meet the Prince, to see him. Finn felt that only the Prince could make this world right again.

On the fourth morning Finn woke up in Bright Water Citadel, the bugles sounded. Finn and Lucky were discussing swords with Gallad the blacksmith in his forge. When the bugles sounded, Lucky shot a concerned look at Finn. They quickly said farewell to Gallad, and raced to the city gates.

As Finn and Lucky ran, Liam the Steward galloped by on horseback with a handful of soldiers. They were heading to the dock.

## ⚜ 15 ⚜

### ELLIS & DILLON

Finn and Lucky chased Liam through the gate. At the giant boulders, they scrambled up for a clear view of the harbor.

Lucky pointed. Finn squinted. Breaking through the fog, a small sailboat inched toward the dock. Atop the main mast hung a checkered flag, another cry for help.

Bright Water's Steward met the ship as it reached the dock. From the rocky pass, Lucky and Finn watched.

Two men step off the ship. Liam approached cautiously. After a few minutes, two of the Steward's soldiers helped the sailors onto horses, and the whole group headed back up the path.

"Quick," Lucky said, grabbing Finn's arm, "we'll

meet 'em at the gate."

Finn and Lucky carefully climbed back down the boulder and ran toward the city gate. Liam and his entourage raced ahead, through the gates and into the courtyard - toward the castle.

"Hurry," Lucky urged.

Finn chased Lucky, chasing Liam. Through raced through the gates, into the courtyard, between the crowds, into the castle, and straight up to Red Beard's bedroom. Lucky and Finn arrived just in time to hear Liam announce the strangers.

"Captain Red Beard," Liam asked in a soft, slightly winded voice, "Two of Lord Emigre's men have travelled far to speak with you."

A murmur rose from the crowd at the door.

*Men from Lord Emigre's Citadel?*

Red Beard sat up in bed.

"Go on, friends. What news have ye of Lord Emigre?"

The two men looked sheepish standing before Red Beard.

Half drenched in salty rags, they held their hats between their hands to honor the wounded Captian.

"Sir, if ye please," the first said, stepping forward, "we thank ye kindly for speaking with us, and we wish ye full health."

"Ay," the second said, stepping forward. "I am Ellis, and this is Dillon, and, we come askin' for your help."

"Go on," Red Beard replied. "Lord Emigre has long been a friend of Bright Water Citadel, and we'll do all in our power to help him, right boys?"

All those in the room answered, "Ay, for the Prince."

"For the Prince," Ellis and Dillon repeated.

"To be honest, sirs, we weren't certain dis Citadel even existed anymore." Dillon started in. "We knew of ye Capt'n, but we've not seen Bright Water ourselves until dis mornin' when we passed through da fog."

"Bright Water Citadel be true indeed," Liam the Steward replied. "Now, about your story?"

"Ay," Ellis nodded. "In the attack, Lord Emigre sent all who would fit into the cellars below the city. Nearly all in the citadel travelled underground to the highlands beyond Albin. We believe they are safe."

"Ay," Dillon added, "but Lord Emigre and his inner circle remained, to lock and hide the cellar entrance."

All those in the room and doorway fell silent as Ellis and Dillon told their story. Even the breeze outside seemed to hold its breath. Little Finn leaned in from the doorway.

Ellis continued, "That wicked Governor sent many men over our walls. He arranged for his fleet to block your Starling in the harbor. Lord Emigre realized we were trapped like birds in a cage."

Dillon picked up the story, "Seeing no opportunity for escape, Lord Emigre sent Ellis and I to hide at the harbor. Two others were sent to hide below the coast at the forest edge. Should any of we four escape, we would find help. The final two remained with Lord Emigre, ready to greet the enemy."

"Lord Emigre gave the orders, and we quickly said our goodbyes," Ellis chipped in, tearing up a bit. "Dillon and I hurried to the harbor, moving among the shadows. We dodged smoke and fire. We arrived at the docks just as soldiers cleared the city walls. There, we hid in a secret place and waited."

Dillon continued, "From our hiding, we could hear cannons firing on the Starling. We feared the worst. After a long wait, we heard soldiers approach the harbor. They lined the dock and waited. So we remained hidden."

"Eventually," Ellis added, "one of the Governor's tall ships entered the harbor and collected the men on the dock."

"The Governor's army destroyed our city," Dillon sighed. "They looted our shops and storehouses. And that tall ship sailed away with everything."

"Ay," Ellis added. "They also loaded our men. We

watched as the two sent to the forest, were marched onto the ship in chains - like common criminals."

"And those with Lord Emigre," Dillon continued, "we watched them march onto the ship in chains."

A murmur of anger swelled in the room as they listened to Ellis and Dillon recount the fall of Lord Emigre's citadel.

"And in the end," Ellis finished, with his head hanging low, "we saw Lord Emigre himself march onto the ship in shackles."

"Disgrace," one man mumbled.

"The Governor's gone too far," said another.

Ellis nodded, "Ay, when the tall ship left our dock and disappeared beyond the mouth of our harbor, we came out from our hiding, secured a small sailboat."

"This place," Dillon added, "Bright Water Citadel, was the only place we could go."

Grumbling in the room quickly grew from murmurs to an angry clamor. All complained against the wicked Governor.

From the bed, Red Beard raised his hand. A hush fell across the room as everyone looked toward the Captain.

"Friends, Lord Emigre remembers the Prince," Red Beard spoke with quiet passion. "Lord Emigre stands alongside Bright Water."

A cheer rang out.

"And," Liam added, "Bright Water Citadel will stand with him.

More cheers, broke out, and many in the room greeted Ellis and Dillon with hugs and hearty hand shakes.

After a few minutes, Captain Red Beard again raised his hand.

The room grew silent.

"Lord Emigre needs our help," he said, this time a bit louder. "Prepare the way, so we may rise up against this false Governor. For too long, he has failed to serve our land."

Leaning on his right elbow, Red Beard raised himself to a seated position. His voice growing stronger with each phrase he spoke.

"For too long, the Governor has ignored his calling - to steward this Kingdom. For too long, he has forgotten the Prince."

Another cheer rose up.

"But we shall remind him."

"Ay," the room cried out, "for the Prince!"

"Go, prepare the Starling," Captain Red Beard commanded the room. "Tonight we will raise the lantern flag. Tonight we sail. We fight for Bright Water - for the Prince!"

The room erupted again with cheers.

Quickly, the crowd left Red Beard's room to prepare the ship for sea.

Freckles, Liam, Lucky, and Lit'le Finn remained. They took seats around Red Beard's bed.

"Captain," Freckles paused. "Is it wise to sail so quickly?"

"We cannot abandon Lord Emigre," Lucky protested.

"Ay," Freckles countered, "but we can do nothing until the capt'in recovers."

"I am recovered," Red Beard interrupted.

"Wit' all due respect, Capt'n," Liam chimed in, "Your wounds cut deep. If ye leave today, ye'll not be much help in battle tonight. Perhaps wait a day? Or a week?"

"I'm sorry friend," Red Beard replied, " There be no time for a full healing. I can stand. I can hold a sword. And, we have little time to waste."

Liam nodded, and hung his head, "I suspected you'd say as much."

"Lord Emigre needs us." Red Beard added. "Almost as much as we need the Prince to return."

"Ay," Lucky and Freckles agreed.

## THE GOVERNOR'S WAR

Meanwhile, far away, beyond the fog and across the dark sea, two figures talked about dark things, in a dark tower, atop a dark castle.

"There is no such place," the governor complained, "we destroyed it long ago."

"And the fog?" a darker voice asked.

The devilish figure made the governor twitch.

*Couldn't he see that the battle was won?* he thought. *The Starling had retreated. If Red Beard had survived, he was in no shape to fight. The plan was nearly complete.*

After a pause, the governor mustered a response, "The fog is merely a hiding place. A rock filled sea to sink that pesky ship.

The Governor paced.

"If you believe that, you are more foolish than I have imagined."

Wasn't it enough that he had taken control of the other citadels, and chased Red Beard into dangerous waters?

The Governor kept his distance from Calamitous.

"What would you suggest?" the governor whined, like a frightened boy.

"I thought you'd never ask," Calamitous replied, a dark smile stretching across his face. "Return to the fog. Find the Starling, and put an end to this rebellion once and for all."

Calamitous paused, letting the thought of victory fill the dark tower. Like feeding candy to a hungry child, Calamitous spoke to the Governor's pride.

Then, in a whisper, he added, "It will be time for you to wear a crown. After all this stewarding, are you not now the rightful king?"

"No!" Mom gasped, interrupting the story.

Grandpa shook his head, "We knew this moment would come."

"What moment?" I asked.

"The governor is but a steward. He has never been the king," grandpa replied.

"But he acts like he's the king," Sissie added.

"That's right," grandpa continued. "And he is acting more and more like a king each day. He is starting to choose what he wants rather than what is best for the kingdom."

"Has the governor's heart grown so dark?" mom asked. "Doesn't he remember what it was like to live under the Prince?"

"It seems he has forgotten," grandpa sighed. "Shall we continue?"

We all nodded.

"Where was I," grandpa whispered as his finger followed lines of text on the glowing page, "ah yes, here we are..."

A WICKED SMILE spread across the the governor's face.

"Yes," he said softly, "Perhaps it is time to take what should have been mine all along."

The governor turned away from Calamitous. I will gather my advisors. You will arrange the guard?

"Of course," Calamitous replied, with a wicked smile of his own.

The governor sent word to gather his advisors. He included delegates from each citadels across the kingdom. All but Lord Emigre's Citadel and they were locked up in the Governor's prison.

"WHAT ABOUT BRIGHT WATER CITADEL?" I interrupted. "Shouldn't they be represented?"

"Yes," mother answered. "But since the Bright Water receded, the people stopped believing that Bright Water Citadel still existed."

"It's become something of a myth to the people of the mainland," grandpa added.

"Is that why Dillon and Ellis said they'd never seen Bright Water before?" Sissie asked.

Grandpa nodded.

"And why the crew of the Fortune said the Prince was a myth?" I added.

"Yes," mother smiled.

Sissie and I smiled too. This story was finally starting to make sense.

"May I continue?" grandpa asked.

We all nodded, and his gaze returned to the book.

ALL OF THE Governor's advisors gathered in a large hall at the center of the castle. The hall *had* been the throne room of the true King many years before.

"Gentlemen," he said, standing as tall as he could on a platform at one end of the hall, "the time has come to re-establish order in our kingdom. For too long, we have allowed Red Beard and his rebellious scalawags to pirate our seas and disrupt our rule."

The advisors and many delegates chattered among themselves at the thought of Red Beard sailing free. Some missed the days of old, while others sought power in the present kingdom.

"For too long, we have allowed the men of Lord Emigre's Citadel to aid these rebellious pirates."

The chatter grew.

"And now, we have captured Lord Emigre."

"Aye," many advisors cheered.

Those who didn't cheer looked around in surprise.

*Lord Emigre captured?* they wondered.

The governor continued, "We have chased Red Beard from his port, and punished his citadel for aiding piracy."

"Aye," some advisors cheered.

Many others remained silent, concerned at the fall of Lord Emigre's Citadel.

"And now, we will move against Red Beard."

"Aye," the advisors cheered.

"We will move against whatever remains of Bright Water Citadel."

A murmur spread among the delegates.

*What remains of Bright Water? Are the rumors true?*

"Destroy the last of Bright Water? one advisor shouted. "That would be an act of war!"

With that, the chatter grew - and spread across the room.

The governor could feel he was losing them.

"Why do you murmur? What do you fear?" he asked.

The murmur grew, ignoring the governor's plea.

*Where is he?* the Governor thought.

"Listen," he called out over the murmur, "together will reunite this broken Kingdom..."

The advisors ignored him. The murmuring continued.

"And I will be your King."

Suddenly, everyone stopped talking.

*The governor wanted the throne?*

Stunned silence hung in the air.

In that moment of silence, a dark figure stepped through the doorway at the back of the hall. Behind him, armed soldiers filed into the room and lined the walls.

*Just in time*, the governor thought.

"As you can plainly see," the governor said with renewed confidence, "we have no king. Our prince has left us."

The advisors, still speechless, slowly realized they were surrounded by the governor's army.

"Our kingdom," the governor continued, "is torn by rebellion and greed. This is our moment to rebuild."

"For the black tower," the guard shouted.

Then another. Then another.

Soon, out of fear, the advisors joined the chant:

"For the black tower!"

The governor smiled, as did Calamitous.

*Soon*, they thought, *the throne will be mine*.

"WE HAVE TO DO SOMETHING," Sissie interrupted.

"Should we warn Finn?" I asked.

The book glowed bright.

"I think that's a yes," Sissie smiled.

Grandpa nodded, and so did mom.

"Alright," I said, looking at the book, "the governor

is coming for Red Beard and the crew. He wants to be King!"

The book flickered again. I glanced around the table, my eyes twinkling and heart pounding. Sissie, Mom, and grandpa shared my excitement.

*We're going to win*, I thought. *We're going to stop Calamitous. We're going to bring Finn and father home.*

"Back to the story?" mom asked with fresh enthusiasm.

"Definitely," Sissie smiled.

Grandpa continued to read.

As THE CHANTING CONTINUED, one advisor noticed a small piece of white paper flittering down from the tall, pitched ceiling. He smiled as it reached him.

The advisor wasn't the only one watching that small piece of paper fall. Calamitous also spotted the falling clue.

With a small wave, the governor quieted the chant. He gave new orders. The advisors were to prepare for battle. Every citadel would join the effort. Soon, they would all unite under the Governor's rule.

After the order, advisors and soldiers scattered to make preparations. While the room emptied, one advisor unfolded the small piece of paper that had fallen from the sky, and read it:

*The governor is coming for Red Beard and the crew.*
*He wants to become the new Prince!*

Calamitous kept his eyes on that advisor. with a wave of his hand, several soldiers joined him and they moved quickly toward the advisor.

Feeling their presence, the advisor turned to face the devilish figure and his armed guard. A wide smile stretched across the advisor's face.

"You?" Calamitous cried out, eyes widening in anger. "It can't be!"

"Oh, it's me alright," the advisor said with a wink and a bow.

"Seize him," Calamitous cried out, but it was already too late.

In a flash of white, the advisor disappeared.

## ❧ 17 ❧

## GATHERING HOPE

"**A** white flash?" Sissie interrupted.

"Indeed," grandpa chuckled.

I glanced at mom smiling across from Sissie.

"What?" I asked. "What do you two know?"

Neither said a word.

"I thought we said no more secrets," I whined.

"Shall we keep reading?" grandpa asked with a smile.

"Fine," Sissie sighed.

Grandpa continued to read.

BACK IN BRIGHT WATER BAY, ship preparations moved quickly.

In short order the Starling looked fit for travel. Nearly all of Bright Water Citadel showed up to see the crew depart, and cheer them as they left.

Red Beard enjoyed a carriage escort to the dock, and with some assistance, made his way onto the Starling and up to the helm. Finn climbed high up a rope ladder on the starboard side. He soaked in the crowd's cheers with a grin spread ear to ear.

Finn knew this adventure was bigger than he ever imagined. The thought of playing even a small part thrilled him.

*What an adventure*, he thought. *What a lucky adventure.*

He smiled as the crowd cheered. Finn raised his eyes toward the sky. The morning sunlight felt warm against his cool cheeks.

That's when he noticed *it* - a small piece of paper falling toward him from the sky.

*Was it a clue? A note from home?* he wondered.

Scrambling around the rope ladder, Finn kept his eyes locked on the small piece of paper as it drifted in the brisk breeze.

Finn followed it left and right as he moved up the ladder toward Scoop in the crow's nest. Reaching out, stretching toward the sea, Finn caught the note in his palm.

Some in the crowd noticed Finn and started to point - watching him navigate the ropes high above the dock.

Hooking one arm around the rope where he hung, Finn carefully unfolded the note between his thumb and forefingers.

He read it in a whisper:

*The governor is coming for Red Beard and the crew.*
*He wants to become King!*

Little Finn's heart skipped a beat.

He read the note again, just to be sure.

His face dropped.

Their mission to free Lord Emigre would only work if it was a secret. They didn't stand a chance against the Governor's fleet in a head on battle.

*I have to do something*, he thought.

Little Finn tucked the note into his pocket. Nimble on the ropes, he climbed down a few rungs.

He spotted a loose line swaying in the breeze between his ladder and the main sail.

Finn took a deep breath and jumped from his rope ladder to the swaying line.

Many in the crowd gasped as they watched.

Little Finn caught the swaying line and held on tight as it carried him toward the main sail.

At just the right moment, Finn let go.

This time the whole crowd gasped.

For a moment, Finn flew, like a trapeze artist, right into the main sail. He disappeared in the billowing sail, slid down the loose canvas, and tumbled onto the deck with a thud.

The crowd roared with excitement.

"You alright mate?" Lucky hollered down from the helm.

"Yes, I mean no," Finn called back. "I mean, you need to see this."

Finn pulled himself from the deck and raced toward the helm.

Lucky hurried down the steps to meet him.

"What's the trouble?"

Lil' Finn handed Lucky the note.

Freckles followed quickly and read the note over Lucky's shoulder.

Lucky looked up with a twinkle in his eyes, "Dis be a gift, arrivin' just in time."

"Ay," Freckles added. "Da Capt'n 'ill know what to do."

"Finn, come with me," Lucky instructed. "Freckles,

gather Liam. We'll be needin' more than Luck if we run into the Governor's fleet."

"Ay," Freckles replied.

The crowd continued to cheer as Freckles headed to the dock and Lucky rushed Finn into the Captain's quarters.

"Captain," Lucky interrupted. "Little Finn's got news about the governor!"

"What news?"

Lucky closed the door to shut out the cheering crowd, as Finn pulled the note from his pocket and handed it to Red Beard.

The Captain carefully unfolded the note and read it silently.

"Well, boys," Red Beard started in, "dis be our destiny."

"I had a feeling you'd say as much," Lucky said with a laugh.

"Whether we sail to victory or defeat," the Captain continued, "We must defend the goodness of Bright Water - for the Prince."

"For the Prince," Finn and Lucky repeated.

"Ay, for the Prince," Liam and Freckles echoed, as they burst through the door. "What'd we miss?"

"We sail to our destiny," Red Beard said again.

"But ye cannot be serious about fightin' today," Freckles argued. "You can hardly stand."

"If not today," Red Beard sighed, "when do ye suggest we be sailin'? It'll be less than two days before the governor's fleet reaches us here."

"He's right," Finn added.

"Then let him come. We can defend this Citadel against his miserable fleet."

"His army be too strong in mumber," Red Beard argued back. "Once the governor docks, his army will overrun the Prince's castle. We cannot let that happen."

"Indeed," Lucky answered. "Dis be our moment of choosing."

Silence fell between them as each realized the weight of this moment.

Liam spoke first saying, "Dis be a brave crew, but ya need not go alone. Da people of Bright Water stand wit' ya. We stand against da governor and wit' the Prince.

"Ay, for the Prince," the all repeated.

"As ye be well awares, we've got a small fleet of our own," Liam went on, "an' it'll only take a few hours to ready the ships. We've got enough able men to sail 'em."

"Even if ye had a dozen Starlings, we'd struggle against the governor's fleet," Freckles said.

"Ay," the Captain replied, "that may be. But some battles are worth fightin' even when ye can't see a way to winnin'."

Finn thought on the Captain's words as they all stood in silence.

"Ay," Little Finn whispered in his best pirate accent. "Dis be a battle worth fightin'."

Lucky and Freckles looked up with a smile. Liam took a deep breath and let it out slow.

Then, the three of them let the Captain rest as they readied the other ships. They would all sail from Bright Water before noon.

## ❧ 18 ❧

### PRISONERS ESCAPE

Across the sea, below the old King's throne room, in the very center of the governor's castle, a flash of white light brightened an otherwise dark and empty passage.

*Now, to find Emigre*, the advisor thought to himself.

He pulled up the hood of his cloak, just to be safe.

The advisor seemed to know his way, winding through the maze-like tunnels that connected the governor's castle to the soldier's barracks and the citadel's prison.

He passed the occasional soldier rushing this way or that to prepare for the governor's war. No one paid much attention to the advisor. He moved quickly, in the shadows.

The governor kept his prison well guarded. The

advisor had expected as much. Without time for a plan, he headed straight to an empty storage room.

*This will do nicely*, he thought to himself, stepping inside and closing the door.

Remembering his own time in the prison, the advisor thought hard about a particular hallway behind the guards. He pictured a particular cell. The cell that used to house his dear, old friend.

In a flash of white light, the storage room was empty again. With a second flash, the advisor found himself behind bars.

"Ah," a familiar voice sighed. "Hello, old friend."

The advisor smiled, "I wasn't sure we'd meet again."

"I'm glad to see you," the prisoner smiled.

The prisoner slowly stood up and dusted his tattered clothes. He held a small roll of paper in his left hand.

"Hello indeed," the advisor said, greeting the frail prisoner with a warm hug. "You're beard has grown since I saw you last."

The old prisoner stepped toward a small window in the prison cell. He pulled a metal pendant from his pocket and hit it lightly against the worn metal bars.

Turning back to the advisor, he whispered, "I imagine it has."

He had striking green eyes that twinkled. He stroked his long beard with a frail and dirty hand.

As the prisoner spoke, a kestrel landed at the window and hopped into the cell.

The advisor watched as the old man slid a rolled paper note into a tiny tube on the kestrel's leg. He stroked the bird's head and whispered to it softly. When he finished speaking, the kestrel turned and flew away.

The advisor watched patiently, in silence.

When the kestrel had left, he asked, "Do you still hear from him?"

"Yes," the prisoner replied. "We pass letters time and again."

"I've not forgotten your stories," the advisor continued, "his stories."

The old prisoner smiled deeply. He was fond of the advisor. A comfortable silence followed. Each quietly remembered their time together in former days.

"Old friend," the prisoner asked, "what has brought you to my darkened corner of this Bright world?"

"Hmm," the advisor complained, "this world has become less bright than I remember."

The old prisoner nodded in agreement.

The advisor continued, "I'm looking for a Lord

who doesn't belong in this prison. Do you know where they are holding Emigre?"

"I do."

"Excellent," the advisor replied. "He is needed."

"There is more?" the old friend asked.

The advisor hesitated, and then nodded, "I need a favor."

"Go on."

"As we speak, the governor prepares for war."

"I have heard."

"But all is not lost."

"Indeed," the prisoner smiled. "Rarely, if ever, is *all* lost."

"Hmm," the advisor sighed. "Even here, you choose hope?"

"I find hope is often the most sensible choice," the prisoner said, his green eyes twinkling.

The advisor smiled, then continued.

"There remains at least one boat that sails under the lantern - that sails for the Prince."

"Who?"

"Red Beard."

"Of course," the old prisoner whispered, tilting his head, deep in thought.

The advisor waited.

"Lord Emigre sits alone in a cell at the end of this hall."

"And the key?" the advisor asked.

"Unguarded, hanging near his cell, also at the end of the hall."

"Thank you, old friend."

"For Bright Water," the old prisoner nodded. "And, the favor you seek?"

"Will you notify him? Will search the Kingdoms, and tell him?"

"Hmm, that is a significant favor," the prisoner's gaze drifted out the window of his cell. "Do you believe it is time?"

"I do," the advisor answered. "The darkest fiend has returned. The governor is his puppet. His darkness now stretches all the way to the fog."

"Perhaps you are right," the prisoner answered. "Perhaps it *is* time, afterall. May the strength of Bright Water go with you."

"And you also," the advisor nodded, "for the prince."

"Always," the prisoner echoed, "for the prince."

The advisor offered a small bow. The old prisoner returned the bow, and both men disappeared in flashes of green and white light.

"WAIT, WHAT?" I interrupted.

Grandpa lifted his head from the book and glanced at me over his glasses.

"A green flash?" I went on.

"Like the Lady of the Western Wood!" Sissie gasped.

"Yeah, that's what I was thinking!" I smiled.

Mom and grandpa glanced at each other.

"I told you they were quick learners," he said with a smile.

"So it *is* the same?" I asked.

"And the white flash," Sissie continued, "That advisor. It's dad, right?"

"I knew it!" I interrupted. "This is awesome!"

Mom and grandpa both chuckled. Finally, things were looking up.

"You too *are* quick learners," mom laughed. "Shall we continue?"

We all nodded. Grandpa slide his glasses back on his nose and returned to the book.

IN ANOTHER FLASH of white light, the advisor stood alone at the end of the dark prison hall. Next to him, a ring of keys hung on the wall. He collected the keys and headed straight to Emigre's cell.

"Lord Emigre," he whispered.

A shadow lifted inside the dim lit cell. A prisoner walked toward the door.

"Your services have been requested elsewhere," he continued.

Lord Emigre's face appeared at the small cell window.

"Charles," he smiled. "What a pleasant surprise. To what do I owe this honor?"

"It's a long story," Charles smiled, anxious to leave the prison. "I'll explain on the way."

"Wait," Lord Emigre said. "I've got good men here. Men who can help."

"I can help, but we must hurry."

Quickly and quietly, they searched for Emigre's men. Two were on the same hall. The other two were in a different wing. No guards patrolled the prison. It seemed all the governor's men were at the docks preparing for war.

Once Emigre's men were freed, Charles led them through the castle undetected, and across the court-yard to the governor's stables.

They stole away on six of the his finest steeds, heading southeast toward Emigre's citadel.

As they crested the first hill, Charles paused to look back. He could see the dark castle perched above the sea. Soldiers, like ants, covered the dock as they loaded supplies. The governor's fleet remained docked in the harbor.

What had seemed impossible just hours before, now seemed possible. The hope of the old prisoner was spreading. Charles could feel it. He looked at Emigre, and Emigre's men.

"For the Prince?"

"Ay," they echoed with a renewed spirit, "For the Prince."

Turning away from the dark castle, they shot across the continent at top speed.

"WE SHOULD TELL FINN!" Sissie interrupted.

"Great idea Sissie," I chimed in, "we should tell him about dad and Emigre!"

The book fluttered with white light. It seemed to agree.

Grandpa and mom nodded with smiles.

"I think that's a great idea," mom said.

Sissie and I looked at each other.

"Go ahead," I nodded, "You take this one – it was your idea first."

A proud grin spread across Sissie's face.

"Okay, thanks."

She turned to the book and spoke in a clear, strong voice:

*Lord Emigre is free. He is heading home. He will fight with you!*

The book flashed bright, and we smiled across the table at each other.

Sissie and I were starting to believe too. Bright Water might be saved after all.

## ❦ 19 ❦

### NEARLY THERE

I t took much of the day for Steward Liam to
gather his men and ready his fleet.

Though just two-thirds the size of the
Governor's tall ships, the Starling floated longer and
taller than any of the other ships in Bright Water
Citadel. She was the last of the original vessels left by
the Prince, to protect Bright Water.

Over the years, the Governor had sunk or
commandeered the other vessels, as he slowly took
over the Kingdom. Those that he commandeered,
now sailed under his banner - the black tower.

Steward Liam's fleet had been built for fishing, not
protecting.

The citizens of Bright Water Citadel spent all
morning loading cannons and light ammunition into

their fishing vessels. Each carried several cannons and a small crew of fighting men.

What they lacked in size and manpower, the people of Bright Water made up for in heart. Fighting for the Prince was a great honor. Despite their poor odds, Steward Liam and his people readied themselves to raise the lantern. They would stand with Captain Red Beard, no matter the cost.

On the deck of the Starling, the crew buzzed with excitement. Soon, they would set sail.

Finn again readied himself on the ropes of the starboard side. He climbed nearly halfway to Scoop.

Freckles still manned the helm and Lucky directed the crew from just outside the Captain's quarters.

Just before they pushed off, Freckles noticed a small, drifting piece of paper.

"Ahoy!" he hollered. "Lit'le Finn!"

Finn spun around. Freckles pointed. Finn followed the angle of Freckle's outstretched arm – up, past the second sail, across to the port side.

He spotted it. Nearly as high as Scoop.

*Another note,* he thought.

He nodded back at Freckles and started climbing. Finn hurried up the ladder, drawing close to the crow's nest. He swung behind the ropes and drew a deep breath, preparing himself. Them, he let it out slow.

Finn gathered his legs, and leapt from one rope ladder to the other - crossing nearly ten feet, high above the ship's deck. He struck the portside rope ladder hard, and slid down a bit before hooking the ladder with his forearm. Finn scrambled to swing his legs into place. He hung more than twenty feet above the deck.

"Hoorah!" Lucky cheered from below. "You're nearly there."

Lucky had spotted the note too.

Next, Finn swung himself to the outside of the rope ladder and scanned the horizon for the clue. He could see it out a bit, and above him. He scurried up a few rungs, leaned out, and reached as far as he could toward the sea.

The paper flittered beyond his grasp, slowly drifting out over the bright blue lagoon.

Finn smiled. He knew what needed to be done. Racing up the ladder toward Scoop, Finn turned again to locate the small floating note.

"What're ye after?" Scoop asked, leaning over the edge of the crow's nest.

Finn squinted up at Scoop with a smile, "I fancy a swim?"

With that, Finn leapt from the ladder, beyond the port side, straight toward the clue. Stretching out his right hand, Finn grabbed the paper and closed his fist tight around it.

A second later Little Finn splashed into the bright blue water.

It was warmer than he expected - the perfect chill to offset Bright Water's afternoon sun.

Lucky and Freckles hurried to the port side rail just in time to see Little Finn surface. He raising his right hand high, still clutching tight to the note. By this time, the whole crew had stopped to watch. They roared with laughter. The crew quickly fished Finn out of the lagoon, and he shook himself dry like a dog.

"Now, about that note," Freckles pressed.

"Right," Finn answered, with a sopping beard now dripping from his chin.

He opened up the note and read it to himself as Lucky and Freckles peered over his shoulders:

*Lord Emigre is free. He is heading home. He will fight with you!*

"Da Capt'n 'ill be wanting' to see dis right away," Lucky said with a grin.

"Perhaps our fortune's be lookin' up afterall," Freckles added with a nod. "You two swashbucklers notify the Capt'n. I'll get Liam.

"Ay," Finn replied, and they hurried off to share the good news.

In the Captain's quarters, Red Beard sat behind his desk, studying maps.

"Capt'n," Finn said, racing ahead of Lucky, "we got another note."

"Emigre is free and with us," Lucky said, following Finn through the door.

"Free?" Red Beard asked looking up.

Finn slapped the note onto Red Beard's desk. The Captain lifted it to the light and squinted the dim lit room. A smile crept across his face.

"Dis be good news, boys," he smiled.

Steward Liam and Freckles joined them, out of breath.

"Good news indeed," Liam echoed. "What be our new plan of attack?"

The five of them studied Red Beard's map, sorted a plan, and readied to shove off. They would travel straight to Lord Emigre's Citadel, join his fleet, and have a fighting chance against the black tower.

"For the Prince?" Red Beard asked.

"Ay, for the Prince," they echoed.

Finn changed into dry clothes, and wrung out his beard.

By supper, they were through the fog, pushing out

into the open sea. The Starling led at a slow pace. She had good wind, but chose not to use it. The Bright Water fishing fleet hadn't been built for speed, and Red Beard's command was clear - they would sail together at all cost.

Throughout the night the sea remained calm, but with dawn, a cool wind swept down from the north. As the morning sun climbed higher in the sky, steady and strong wind continued to press south.

Red Beard worried that the wind would speed the Governor's attack. By noon, Scoop confirmed the Captain's worry. Still hours from Lord Emigre's citadel, Scoop spotted vessels far off. Mere dots on the horizon to the northwest.

"Ahoy?" he hollered from the crow's nest. "Dar be vessels approachin'."

Freckles held firm at the helm. Lucky hurried into the Captain's quarters where Red Beard shared stories of adventure with Finn.

"Capt'n," Lucky started. "Yer fears be right. Scoop's spotted vessels approachin' from de nort'."

Red Beard sighed, "We still be too far from Lord Emigre?"

"Ay," Lucky shrugged, "half a day."

"Then dis be our moment," Red Beard said with resignation. "We shall perform our solemn duty. We are the last guardians and protectors of our Bright Waters."

Lucky bowed his head, "Indeed, Capt'n. Dis be our moment. Has been an honor to serve wit ye."

"For the Prince," Red Beard said, rising from his desk.

"For the Prince," Lucky echoed. "I'll ready da crew."

Red Beard nodded, and Lucky hurried to the deck.

Finn looked up concerned.

"Strap on ye sword, Lit'le Finn," the Captain said with a fresh twinkle in his eyes. "Today, ye be writin' yer own adventure."

## ❦ 20 ❦

## SURRENDER OR SINK

Finn relayed Red Beard's orders to Freckles at the helm. They guessed the governor's fleet would be close enough to attack just before sunset.

Lucky signaled commands to Steward Liam and the rest of their fleet. They Bright Water Fleet continued to sail west, and the fishing vessels positioned themselves southeast of the Starling. She would cover them as long as she could.

Each ship prepared their cannons, battened down hatches, and prepared for the coming battle. Each ship raised their lantern banner high.

All the while, the Governor's fleet inched closer.

As the sun crept toward the horizon, the first cannon shots broke the peaceful silence. Water splashed before and behind the Starling. The governor's fleet sailed six ships strong.

His fleet spread wide, cutting angling before and behind the Starling and her fleet of fishing vessels. More cannonballs splashed around them - warning shots. The Starling and her fleet slowed. They were blocked on three sides, by a near circle of tall ships slowing into position.

Red Beard stood, tightened the dressing on his wound, and slipped into his Captain's jacket.

"Lit'le Finn," he said. "When we first met, ye said ye be lookin' for adventure."

Finn looked up, nervous, but excited.

"I believe ye be findin' it," Red Beard added with a twinkle in his bright blue eyes.

"Ay," Finn nodded. "An adventure for the Prince."

"For the Prince," Red Beard repeated. Then he added, "Be brave, but be not foolish. Hope is never lost."

With that, he left the Captain's quarters and walked toward Lucky at the bow. Finn headed to Freckles at the helm. His heart raced as he took in the scene. The Governor's tall ships surrounded their tiny fleet.

The governor and Calamitous stood side by side on the center ship.

"Is this your army?" the governor shouted at the Starling. "Surrender now, and I will be merciful. I will spare the fishermen."

Echoing laughter rose in all directions. The governor's army mocked Red Beard from every side.

"We sail by the lantern. We fight for the Prince. We'll not be surrenderin' this day," Red Beard called back.

Chants and cheering rose up from the Bright Water fleet, "For the Prince!"

The governor shook his head in disgust.

"You said I had no heart," he mocked, "Yet you would sacrifice your fleet to save your ship Starling?"

With that he raised his arm.

At that command, cannons fired from the Governor's ships - all taimed at the Bright Water fishing fleet. The Starling fired back, and the fishing fleet tried to return fire.

Red Beard's navy was sorely outmatched. Sailors abandoned several badly damaged boats, swimming toward neighboring ships.

"Enough!" Red Beard called above the firing.

The governor lowered his arm, and the firing ceased.

When the sounds of war subsided, only two of Steward Liam's six boats remained afloat. The others sank quickly below the dark water, as their crews called out for rescue.

Red Beard's men cast ropes into the sea, and jumped in to save the men of Bright Water. Sopping, the survivors made their way to one of the three remaining boats.

*We just need more time*, the Captain thought.

The governor enjoyed his drawn out victory.

"Would you like to reconsider?" he asked, still mocking Red Beard and his rag tag sailors.

"What do ye want?" Red Beard called back.

The governor stepped forward, savoring the moment.

"Well," he went on, "I am to become your king."

Cheers rose from across the governor's fleet. Then the cheers turned to chants, "Long live the King!"

After a few moments, the governor waved his hands to quiet the chant.

"You ask what I want? What I want is this. You will surrender. You will hand over the white light. From this day forward, you will serve me - your new king. This rebellion of yours is over."

When he finished, more cheers rang out across the governor's fleet.

"R ED  B EARD  WILL  NEVER  AGREE  to that!" I inter-rupted. " He can't. He just can't."

"If he doesn't," Sissie chimed in, "they'll all be sunk!"

Grandpa sat back to think for a moment. Mom leaned in.

"I thought our clue would do the trick," she sighed. "I really thought they'd make it in time."

"Isn't there something we can do?" I pleaded.

"We can't let them get Little Finn," Sissie added, in a shaky voice.

"No dear," mother said softly, "We certainly can't."

"Shall we continue?" grandpa asked gently.

We all nodded, grandpa found his place, and read on.

W HILE  THE  GOVERNOR'S  men cheered, Finn tugged at Freckles coat to get his attention. When Freckles looked ove, Finn nodded toward the crow's nest, raising his eyebrows.

Freckles took the hint. He tried to followed Finn's glance - up, past the sail, all the way up to the crow's nest. That's when he saw Scoop. A smile crept across Freckles' face.

"Go tell the Captain," he whispered to Finn.

Full of excitement, Finn hurried across the deck. He wove his way past sopping sailors to the bow where Lucky and Red Beard stood firm facing the governor.

Finn whispered his secret to Lucky and Red Beard.

A smile crept across their faces too.

The Captain waited for the cheering to quiet. When it did, he shouted back at the governor:

"An' what of me and me crew?"

Red Beard was buying time.

"What, you ask is the punishment for pirates?" the governor mocked. "Perhaps, you will beg your king for mercy?"

Again, his army roared with laughter, cheering on the governor.

For his part, the governor enjoyed the attention. For so many years, he had been just a governor. A steward of someone else's land.

He had long dreamed of this moment - the time he would finally put an end to Red Beard, and taking the crown.

The devilish figure by the governor's side grew impatient.

"What are you waiting for?" Master Calamitous growled. "Sink them all."

The governor shivered at the sound of the devilish man's voice.

"Enough talking," the governor shouted. "Surrender or sink."

Both crews fell silent, waiting for Red Beard's reply. Before he could answer, the wind carried a faint bugling into earshot.

A murmur began between the men on the governor's ships. What was that sound? Then, a call came from their crow's nests:

"Ahoy," came the warning. "Ships be approachin'."

The governor pulled a scope from his jacket pocket.

A cheer went up from the Starling's crew and the two fishing boats that remained. The bugling continued, growing louder.

"Emigre!" Lucky exclaimed. "And, just in time."

The scope confirmed it, Lord Emigre had arrived, and he brought his fleet. Surprised, the governor hollered a string of commands - pulling back his fleet.

As he did, Red Beard countered - signaling Freckles and Steward Liam to open their sails and fire on the governor's fleet at will.

## ❧ 21 ❧

### FINN'S WIN

**M**aster Calamitous was furious. In a flash of red, he disappeared. This time, Red Beard was ready. Sword drawn, he waited for the second flash.

In a swirl of red, Calamitous appeared center deck on the Starling. The crew scattered away from his reach. The devilish figure stood tall, dagger outstretched, looking for Red Beard.

"I've worked too long to miss this ending," he shouted. "Red Beard, show yourself!"

Cannons firing, smoke clouded the deck of the Starling.

"Where are you Captain? It's high time I finish what I started."

Freckles, Lucky, Red Beard, and Finn all slowly

paced toward the man in the dark cloak. They formed a cautious circle beyond the reach of his staff and dagger.

As the smoke cleared, Calamitous saw that he was surrounded.

"Steady boys," Lucky called out.

Finn could feel a shake in his knees. He hadn't imagined himself facing off with Master Calamitous.

"You've got your grandfather's eyes, boy," Calamitous chided Finn. "Pity he couldn't be here to face me himself..."

Finn felt his face flush red.

"...what kind of coward sends a child to fight in his place?"

"The insult stung. His grandfather was no coward."

"Watch yer tongue," Red Beard countered, stepping forward. "Ye be standin' on me ship now."

Freckles and Lucky inched closer, swords out.

Finn also stepped forward, sword raised. He felt angry. This man was wicked - stirring chaos and confusion.

Calamitous swung his staff and dagger aimlessly, spinning left and right. Turning toward Finn, he shouted.

"This won't be the end, boy. It's barely the beginning."

Calamitous swing around and stabbed at Freckles. Turning more, he swung by Lucky and Red Beard who both stepped back.

Locking eyes with Finn again, he growled, "You tell him I said that."

Then, looking up, the devilish figure shouted.

"Do you hear me?" he screamed into the sky. "This is just the beginning!"

GRANDPA SET the book down and stood up.

"Dad, stop!" mother shouted, grabbing his wrist.

Sissie and I gasped, watching grandpa nearly throw himself into the book.

Mother quickly flipped the book closed and slide it to me.

Grandpa crumbled back into his seat. His cheeks fuming red, and his hands shaking.

"That wicked, old fool," grandpa muttered under his breath. "How dare he talk to my grandson like that."

"He's just a scared coward, caught in his own schemes,"mother added, now gently rubbing grandpa's back. "How about I read for a little while. I think our part is nearly finished."

"Yes dear," grandpa said, turning to his tea. "I think that's probably best."

Mother nodded, and I slid the closed book back to her.

She lifted the edges and let it fall open on its own. The pages flittered forward and back, settling into a soft glow in the latter half of the book.

Mother scanned the page.

"Here we are," she said softly. "Shall I continue?"

We all nodded, and grandpa took a long sip of his tea.

Mother began to read.

"Do you hear me?" he screamed into the sky. "This is just the beginning!"

Finn's eyes narrowed. He fixed his gaze on the tall man in the dark cloak.

*I am no child*, Finn thought. *This is my adventure.*

With a shout, Finn lunged at the devilish figure, and slashed with his sword, shouting, "Don't call me boy!"

The spark of courage surprised the devilish figure. He recoiled, nearly falling to the deck.

Little Finn jabbed, and his sword cut into Calamitous just above the knee.

Calamitous screamed, and in a swirl of red light, he disappeared. Finn fell to the deck where Calamitous had been.

The crew looking on cheered wildly.

Lucky, Freckles, and Red Beard stepped toward Finn and helped him to his feet. He smiled wide as he returned the sword to its sheath.

Around then, the cannon smoke had cleared. Lord Emigre's fleet now filled the horizon. Still bugling, they raced north, sailing after the Governor's retreating fleet.

Lord Emigre himself stood at the helm of his lead ship.

"For the Prince!" he called to them from the helm.

"For the Prince!" they echoed back.

Cannons firing, Lord Emigre continued to pursue the black tower fleet. With nowhere to hide, it seemed the Kingdom would soon have a new governor.

Red Beard recognized another face on Emigre's boat. A man standing center deck, eyes fixed on the Starling.

That man disappeared in a flash of white. Finn saw him too.

With a second flash, that man landed beside Finn,

center deck where Calamitous had been. Finn threw his arms wide and tackled him.

"Easy little one," the man laughed, catching Finn and falling to the deck.

Finn smiled, holding tight to father.

"We did it, dad!" he said. "We really did it!"

Charles smiled wide, hugging Finn on the deck.

"We did indeed," he laughed. "Well done, little one. Well done."

Freckles and Lucky stepped close and helped Charles to his feet. Finn scrambled up too, still holding close to his father.

"Charles," Red Beard said stepping forward to hug father, "Ye must be very proud'a yer boy."

"Ay," Charles said with a smile. "Very proud indeed."

Turning to Finn, the Captain smiled wide again. His blue eyes twinkled.

"Well laddy, did ye find the adventure ye be lookin' for?"

"Ay, Capt'n," Finn smiled.

"Ye always be welcome in Bright Water," Red Beard went on. "Perhaps, you'll even meet the Prince on yer next visit."

"For the Prince," the cheer rose up from the deck.

Finn threw a hearty hug around the Captain, who winced a bit, still recovering from his wound.

"T'anks," Finn said.

"Ay," Red Beard said with a smile.

Finn gave hugs to Freckles and Lucky next, told them how very much he wanted to stay. They agreed and reminded him that always had a place on the Starling.

Then, it was time. Finn stepped back toward father and turned to face his mates. Tears welled up in his eyes.

With a final wave, and a flash of light, Charles and Finn disappeared.

Red Beard headed back to the helm, and started barking orders. In a moment, the Starling had turned to chase Lord Emigre, with Steward Liam following.

SUDDENLY, an explosion of light filled the basement.

All four of us stood from the table, ready to greet father and Finn. When the light cleared, they were with us.

"Did you guys see that?" Finn shouted, still brimming with excitement.

"Every brave moment," grandpa smiled. "Every brave moment little one."

We sat in the basement for the rest of the day. Little Finn wanted to retell every moment, while father and mother added details from their time at the tower, and with Emigre.

Grandpa listened as Sissie and I told father about our other adventures, as little Finn listened from mother's lap.

When all our story telling came to a close, father looked toward grandpa and mother.

"I think it's time."

"I believe you're right Charles," grandpa smiled, the twinkle returning to his eyes.

"Yes," mother added with a smile, "they are ready."

# EPILOGUE

This marks the end of our earliest adventures - our beginnings, or origin as story keepers.

Looking back, I can see how grandpa used each story to train us.

I'll never forget that first night - when grandpa introduced me to Drift. It seems like ages ago. Back when we read stories for fun.

Over time, we've realized the stakes are much higher than we first imagined. Don't get me wrong, we still have fun - and lots of it.

In those early stories, we started learning about the power of story keeping - and the limits. We started to learn what you can and can't do to change a story.

And he had good reason to train us. We quickly

learned why stories need protecting. Dark forces worked hard to destroy these books.

The maps and pictures in grandpa's basement also told a story. Places where these books were sold. People that could flash like us.

Despite our training, we had many more questions than answers. There were others passing in and out of these stories - flashing with other colors.

We wanted - we needed - to learn more about the old prisoner in the dark tower, and the Lady of the Western Wood.

We needed to learn more about Master Calamitous, Lark, and Devlin. Who they really are, and why they work so hard to destroy these stories.

But I'm getting ahead of myself. All of this makes sense when you hear it in the proper order. One story at a time - that's what father always says.

So for now, this is the end. The end of our beginning.

## THANKS FOR READING THE STORY KEEPING SERIES

## A REMINDER & REQUEST

1. Don't forget to download the audio version for free https://storykeeping.carrd.co
2. Will you please leave a review? Besides putting a smile on my face, they help other readers find this book. Thanks!

## ABOUT THE AUTHOR

Who doesn't love a good story?

My parents wove incredible tales at bedtime and around campfires. I caught my mom's passion for writing pretty early. The result? A wild imagination.

I write to ignite imagination in my own kids and other readers.

The *Story Keeping Series* captures the excitement I remember from bedtime stories. As Riles, Sissie, and Finn jump under the sheets in their bunks, I can see the quilt on my childhood bed. As they hang on grandpa's every word grandpa, I can see mom or dad at the foot my bed reading to my brother and I.

Grandpa guides and mentors these young heroes, teaching them to save the happy ending - it's the art of story keeping. The twists and turns will "tickle the hair in your ears."

How'd I end up spinning these tales?

A few standout teachers - Mrs. Orona (4th), Mrs. Avery (11th), and Dr. Joliff (undergrad) - tricked me into thinking I could do anything - especially write. It's taken years for the stories grown in my mind to find their way into pages. As they do, they grow again - characters choosing their own way.

I've loved this partnering - between my own ideas, and the lives my characters take on. They live in a world similar to mine - where good and evil battle for the hearts and minds of us all. As the children work to save each book, I learn about their place in this broader battle - to become heroes who make a difference in a broken world.

Like Riles, I want to be a little more heroic when the sun sets.

How about you? Want to be heroic?

What's stopping you?

BOOKS BY A R MARSHALL

**STORY KEEPING SERIES**

Book 1, The Night I Became A Hero

Book 2, The Night We Met A Dragon

Book 3, Secrets Beyond the Nile

Book 4, Dark Water Pirates

Made in the USA
Monee, IL
29 October 2022

16807542R00105